P O D

POD

STEPHEN WALLENFELS

namelos

Copyright © 2009 by Stephen Wallenfels
Printed in the United States of America
Designed by Michael Wallenfels
First edition

Library of Congress Cataloging-in-Publication Data
Wallenfels, Stephen.
Pod / Stephen Wallenfels. — 1st ed.
p. cm.
Summary: As alien spacecraft fill the sky and zap up any
human being who dares to go outside, fifteen-year-old
Josh and twelve-year-old Megs, living in different cities,
describe what could be their last days on Earth.
ISBN 978-1-60898-011-6 (hardcover : alk. paper)
ISBN 978-1-60898-010-9 (paperback : alk. paper)
[1. Science—Fiction. 2. Fiction.] I. Title.
PZ7.W158864 Po 2009
[Fic]—dc22
2008029721

n a m e l o s
www.namelos.com

For Teresa and Michael

CONTENTS JOSH

POD

"In our obsession with antagonisms of the moment we

often forget how much unites all the members of humanity.

Perhaps we need some outside, universal threat to make

us recognize this common bond. I occasionally think how

quickly our differences worldwide would vanish if we were

facing an alien threat from outside this world."

PRESIDENT RONALD REAGAN,
addressing the United Nations General Assembly,
September 21, 1987.

- STATIC -

The screeching wakes me.

Like metal on metal tearing and twisting and amplified a thousand times. I spring up in bed and clamp my hands over my ears. But my brain feels like it's being pushed from the inside out. The sound goes on and on, building and building. I stagger out of bed and collapse. I want to twist my head off, the pain is so big. There's only one thing to do. I scream, hoping it will drown out the sound that is killing me in my room in the dark.

And it stops.

I tense up, ready for another blast, but it doesn't come. A soft, deep hum fills my throbbing head. I stand, using the wall to steady my legs. Just as I'm thinking What the hell, the hall light turns on. Seconds later my door bangs open. Dad leans hard against the frame, his breathing short and fast. He's been wearing a pacemaker since Thanksgiving. This had better not be a heart attack.

"You okay, Josh?" he asks.

His voice is shaky, but not like he needs CPR.

"My head hurts," I say.

"Yeah. My ears are still ringing."

He waits, then says, "Can I come in?"

"Sure," I say, snagging a pair of sweatpants off the floor and sliding them over my boxers. "Just don't trip on anything." A sweatshirt hangs over the back of my computer chair. I put it on.

Dad hits the lights and navigates through the minefield of clothes, burned CDs, gaming magazines, and assorted AV cables on his way to the window. He's wearing red pajama bottoms and a white T-shirt. A wet spot with a couple of brown chunks stains the front of his shirt. Based on the smell that hits me as he walks past, I figure it's the digested version of last night's supper. He peers out at the dawning day and scratches his butt. I'm sure he's calculating barometric pressure and cloud cover. To me it's obvious—another spring morning, more wind, more rain.

"What just happened?" I ask.

"Don't know."

"A car crash?"

Still looking out the window, he says, "No. This took too long. It was something else."

"Like it was inside your head?"

He turns from the window. "Exactly."

"Then what the hell was it? I thought my brain was exploding."

"I'm thinking a furnace bearing."

That seems like a huge stretch. I walk to my desk and pick up the handset for the landline. No dial tone. Since our phone and Internet are bundled together, that means no web. Perfect. How will I get the rest of my homework done?

I say, "Can furnace bearings shut down the telephone?"

"It's just a theory," he says, sitting on a corner of my bed.

Strength is returning to my legs. The ringing in my ears is almost gone. I glance at the digital clock on my nightstand.

5:03.

I should be sleeping for another hour. Then it's thirty minutes of cramming for a first-period history test, but I can't get online for the notes. This day has suck written all over it. A thought floats by, something I should catch, but my aching brain can't reel it in.

Dad says, "Try the radio."

I switch it on. Nothing but static up and down the band. And it's a weird, wavering screechy static. I try AM. More of the same. The sound reminds me of the big noise. I turn it off. It's a good thing Mom's away at a conference. Otherwise she'd be freaking out about now.

I'm starting to feel uneasy, like I'm on the edge of something but not sure what. I track down yesterday's jeans and dig out my cell. "How much you want to bet this doesn't work?" I flip open the phone, dial our home number. "No service," I say.

"This is definitely unusual."

"You think?"

12

He shoots me a pained look.

"With a noise like this," I say, "shouldn't Dutch be barking his head off?"

"Maybe."

"I'm going to see if he's all right."

Dad stands up. "I'll check the furnace."

Downstairs the house is dark, but there's enough early morning light to see where I'm going. I walk into the living room first, look out the picture window. We live on a quiet cul-de-sac with overgrown hedges and washed-out cedar fences. At this hour the neighborhood should be mostly asleep, but it isn't. Lights are on everywhere. The apartment building across the street is lit up like it's dinnertime, not two hours before breakfast. I guess we aren't the only ones with squeaky bearings.

I walk into the kitchen. It still has the lingering smells from last night's supper—Dad's regrettable attempt at French onion soup. The digital clock on the microwave reads 5:05. Again that slippery thought comes to me, but this time I'm able to hold on. It's probably been five minutes since the big noise. I wonder if it happened at exactly 5:00. I'm sure that means something, but again, the significance is just out of reach.

Dutch is sleeping on the back deck, curled up on his rug by the patio door. A nervous, sad-eyed mutt, he barks at everything, even squirrels in a tree. I tap on the glass. He opens an eye, flips his tail a couple of times, and settles back to sleep. This feels wrong.

Dad walks into the room and stands beside me. "I guess Dutch didn't hear it," he says, yawning. His tone doesn't match the unsettled feeling in my stomach.

"But none of the neighborhood dogs are barking."

Dad scratches his head.

"How's the furnace?"

"Running like a champ."

We share a look but say nothing.

Birds fly from branch to branch. A gust of wind sends leaves skittering across the patio floor. Storm clouds gather and darken a turbulent sky. The sun feels like it's going down instead of up. Sirens pierce the moment. It's an ambulance and a fire truck, somewhere close. This wakes Dutch. He sees us, jumps to his feet, presses his nose to the glass.

I reach for the door.

"Josh, wait!"

The urgency in Dad's voice stops me cold. He's looking up. I follow his eyes.

The air is sucked out of my lungs. My jaw hangs open, numb.

Dropping down through the clouds, silent like a spider on a web, is a massive black sphere.

It's a mile away at least, but even from this distance it dwarfs the neighborhoods below. I brace myself for the horror of watching houses crushed with people inside. But it stops well above the trees, maybe five hundred feet off the ground. It hovers soundlessly.

Dad whispers, "Sweet Jesus."

He points to another one, farther to the east. Then another.

Within half a minute the entire horizon is dotted with black spheres. Dutch scratches at the glass, oblivious to the scene playing out above his head.

The spheres begin to rotate.

Then, as if on cue, they all start emitting jagged beams of white-blue light. The beams split off into smaller and smaller ones, like twigs off a branch, some into the air, most striking the ground. Two cars are speeding down a fire road on Horse Heaven Hills. A flash of light and they're both gone. No explosion, no ball of flame. Just gone.

"Dad!" I yell.

He stares out the window, shaking his head, mumbling, "No, no, no."

"I'm checking out front!"

I sprint through the kitchen and down the hall to the living room window. I scan the front yard. There's a sphere spinning above the apartment building. It's picking off cars parked along the curb. A dog trots by, dragging an empty leash.

There's a bicycle on its side in the middle of the cul-de-sac, an upside-down helmet, and rolled-up newspapers scattered around. These belong to Jamie, our newspaper girl.

I open the front door. Search our yard, the street.

"Jamie!"

Nothing.

"Jamie!"

To my right, a whimpering, crying sound. Four cars and a beat-up RV are parked at various spots in the cul-de-sac. A white Honda is closest to me. Jamie is crouched down low, using her position to shield her from the sphere. It's a forty-yard dash to our front step.

A flash of light and two cars are gone.

"Jamie, now!"

She looks at me. There's a cut on her forehead, blood smeared on her cheek.

Another flash. The RV disappears.

She hesitates for a second, then stands up and runs. But something is wrong. Her left leg collapses. She regains her balance, starts running, stumbles again. I lunge to go out and help her. Two arms wrap me in a vise from behind. I'm pulled, screaming, back into the house.

Jamie is at the end of our driveway. Her eyes lock on mine.

She disappears, mid-stride, in a flash of blue-white light.

- FLASHES OF LIGHT -

She's trying to wake me. "Megs? C'mon, honey."

I'm trying to ignore her.

"Megs. Wake up."

Ignoring Mom is like ignoring a bad itch. She shakes my sleeping bag.

"Wake up, honey. C'mon!"

I know she won't stop. And if I keep it up she'll get mad, and that's something I definitely want to avoid. I open my eyes. "Okay, okay! I'm up already."

She peers at me from the front seat, her face all perfect with Cinnamon Blush lips, brown eyeliner, hair brushed and tied back like she's been at it for hours. Her blue satin top shows more boobs than I thought she had. I sniff the air. Her flowery perfume mixes in with all the dirty laundry piled up on the floor in back.

"Megs, I'm sorry, but I need to get going."

Going? Now I'm wide awake.

"Where?" I sit up in the back seat, rub the sleep out of my eyes, and look at the digital clock duct-taped to the dashboard. It's hard to focus in the dim light.

4:48 a.m.

"Why are we getting up now?"

"I know it's early, honey. I'm sorry. But I'm in a hurry and we have to talk."

Mom saying she's sorry twice in the same day? That's a record. Something is definitely wrong. I need to figure some things out. We're in a place I don't recognize, full of shadows. There's lots of concrete. A blue car is parked next to us, and somewhere beyond that is a green door that reads HOTEL LOBBY.

"Where are we?"

"We're in the parking garage –"

"At a hotel?"

"Yes. But I—"

"I thought we were going to sleep at the beach."

"We ran out of gas, remember?"

It's coming back to me in pieces. Rolling into LA after midnight. The tank on "E." Getting lost. Finding this hotel. Mom parking in the garage, fixing her hair in the mirror, putting on lipstick, going in to get directions to the beach. Me falling back to sleep. Mom kissing me good night, smelling of cigarettes and beer.

"Why do you have to leave now? Why are you all dressed up?"

"That's what I'm trying to tell you. I have a job interview and I need to go right now."

"A job interview?" My heart skips a beat. "In those clothes?"

"Yes, honey. Now you need to listen."

And the missing piece falls into place. The whispering man.

"You're meeting him, aren't you? The one I heard you whispering with outside the car?"

"He bought us dinner," she says, her eyes avoiding mine.

"Buffalo wings?"

I remember them making out. He had thin gray hair and a beard.

She takes a deep breath, fusses with a link on her bracelet. I can tell she's dying to light a cigarette. She leans forward, suddenly going from soft to hard. Her green eyes drill into mine.

"I don't have time for this, Megs. You got that? Now be quiet and listen. You need to do exactly what I tell you."

She pauses, letting her words sink in. I sit in my sleeping bag, stewing.

"Wait in the car. Don't go anywhere. Keep the doors locked and don't open them for anyone. Not anyone. Understand?"

"Not even the police?"

She blinks. This hits a nerve. The police are not our friends at the moment. "I'll only be gone an hour," she says.

"A whole hour! Where are you going?"

"A different hotel."

"Why doesn't he interview you in this hotel?"

"This hotel doesn't have a...coffee shop."

She's making absolutely no sense. "A coffee shop? What kind of job is it?"

A car pulls up behind us. It's a white Mercedes with tinted windows. I can't see who's driving, but I know it's the whispering man. She grabs her purse.

"Why don't we just go to San Diego now?" I ask, knowing I can't stop her but needing to try. "We can just—"

"Honey, please. We don't have any gas, remember?" She smiles. We're back to soft. "Don't turn on the radio, okay? You could kill the battery and God knows we don't need that. And remember, stay...in...the...car. When I come back I'll have some money. We can buy gas and a huge breakfast at Denny's, okay?" I hear the Mercedes idling behind us. She leans over the seat, kisses my hair, and whispers, "And then we'll go to the beach. I promise." Her perfume hangs like a cloud of rose petals over my head. She checks her lips in the rearview mirror, tugs her blouse down, opens the door, and leaves.

She starts walking toward the Mercedes, the click of her high heels echoing on the concrete walls. Then she stops, turns around.

She changed her mind!

She hurries back to the car and taps the window. "Lock it," she mouths, pointing to the button. I push it down and she smiles. Her bright red lips blow me a kiss. There's something in her eyes, a glistening wetness, that doesn't match her smile. Whatever this "interview" is, I know she doesn't want the job.

Just because I'm twelve doesn't mean I'm stupid.

I swing around to watch through the duct-taped cracks in the rear window as she walks to the Mercedes. Even in a dirty parking garage she's beautiful. Tall, thin, like a princess—in a clingy red skirt. She opens the passenger door, says something to the driver. He has gray hair and a beard. Without looking back, she gets in. The Mercedes glides out into the early morning shadows.

Now what?

I'm wide awake. I have to pee but my orders are to stay...in...

18

the...car. That's just great. If I'm going to make it I need a distraction. Some kind of game. I'm good at keeping track of time in my head. I can look at a clock once and then know exactly when fifteen minutes has passed, give or take five seconds. My best friend, Jessica, says it's almost creepy the way I always know what time it is. She calls it my "brain clock." It's the closest thing I have to a superpower. I decide to count down each minute until she gets back. That's fifty-nine starting...now.

4:58.

I look around our ratty old car, a '78 Nova with thumb-sized cracks in the dashboard. The ashtray overflows with smashed-up Marlboros with red lipstick on them. Three days' worth of empty Jalapeño Doritos bags are crumpled on the floor. I'm in a sleeping bag that hasn't been washed since who knows when. Mom just sleeps under a thin yellow blanket with cigarette holes. Actually, I wonder if she sleeps at all.

4:59.

I try to remember where we slept two nights ago.

Oh yeah, a truck stop just over the California state line. Smelled diesel fumes all night. But it wasn't as scary as this place. There were more lights. Here there are lots of cars and lots of dark shadowy places between them. I notice a big black SUV in the corner, two rows over. It's so big it makes the car beside it look like a toy. I wish we had a car like that. There'd be so much room...

5:00.

A thousand screaming demons explode in my head.

It finally stops. My whole body is shaking. The car feels like it's spinning and my ears hurt. I don't know what to do, so I bury my head in my sleeping bag and hope that it doesn't happen again. Where's Mom? Why me? Am I sick? All these questions are flooding my brain—when there's another noise.

Sirens.

Not just a couple. Hundreds. I sit up and look around. There are flashes of light, like lightning only without the thunder. Even though

Mom said not to, I turn on the radio. It's just static, no matter what button I push. Then people start running into the parking garage.

First one or two, then a wide-eyed flood. Men in pajamas, women in nightshirts dragging their sobbing kids. A guy wearing only a T-shirt and boxers unlocks the blue car next to ours. He comes out with a gun, sprints to the exit ramp, and starts shooting at the sky. He disappears in a flash of light. Cars start, engines roar. People are trying to leave and other people are trying to stop them. A mom with her two young kids, a boy and girl, run toward the SUV. The little girl drops her stuffed rabbit. She tries to go back, but her mother picks her up and throws her crying into the SUV.

Horns mix with the sirens.

A man trips and falls to the ground.

Cars drive over him like he's a speed bump. I yell at them to stop, but no one hears me. Then the sound of breaking glass, tearing metal—more people screaming. Cars screech down from the upper levels and ram into cars on the ground floor. The SUV is trying to back out of its parking spot. A speeding truck clips the rear fender, crashing it sideways into another car. Now it's trapped. Moments later the mom and her kids spill out the passenger side. Blood is streaming down the little girl's forehead. The mom looks toward the exit. Cars drive out, one after another, and disappear in flashes of light. A red BMW slams on its brakes. It skids halfway into the street and disappears. The mom picks up the girl and they run for the lobby door. The boy stops and turns like he forgot something, but his mom grabs his arm and pulls him away. His face is twisted in a scream.

I smell burning rubber, engine exhaust, gasoline—and then I feel something.

A warm wetness spreads inside my sleeping bag.

Tears stream down my face, they smear on the glass. I feel like I can't breathe. The sounds outside swallow up everything, even the air. I curl up into a ball on the back seat and close my eyes so tight they hurt. But I still see it—cars driving over the fallen man. And those awful blinding flashes.

- MEGAPHONE MAN -

I call them PODs, short for Pearls of Death. They're pearls because they remind me of a pair of dangly earrings I bought Mom for
Christmas last year. Each earring had a single pearl—round, smooth,
and inky black. They weren't very big, but if you looked at them just
right they seemed to shine with a mysterious, translucent light. The
PODs, if you look at them long enough with a pair of binoculars,
seem to have something going on inside them, too. I see shadowy
shapes. Dad says there's nothing to see but space metal.

As for the death part—all I have to do is close my eyes. I see
Jamie's face, eyes open wide, mouth frozen in a silent scream. She
was there, then she wasn't. Like she was deleted.

We counted the PODs today after breakfast. I got one hundred
twenty-eight. Dad got one hundred twenty-two. He wears glasses
and I don't, so there's part of your margin for error. Another vari-
able is, a cloud moves on the horizon and, by golly, there's another
POD. They don't seem to change their position, so that helps. We
agree to split the difference. Dad writes it down in a notebook:
May 15 / 8:55 a.m. – 125 PODs.

I shake my head. We're sitting at the breakfast table, the you-
know-whats spinning silently outside the window. Dutch is inside,
dozing by the patio door.

"How long are we doing this counting?" I ask.

"Every day."

"And the point of this exercise is?"

"Track the changes."

"Why?"

"Maybe figure something out."

"Like what?"

He's drawing an X and a Y axis, labeling them *Days* and *PODs*.
He writes 125 at the bottom of the vertical axis.

"Like what?" I ask again.

"Their next move."

"Their next move? C'mon, Dad!" I slap the breakfast table with my hand, rattling plates and tipping over a saltshaker. White granules spill onto the table. "I'll save you some time, okay? Their next move is to crush us like, like *freaking* bugs." I almost dropped the F-bomb. It was right there, on the tip of my tongue. But he never swears, so I resist the urge in front of him.

"We don't know that," he says.

"Right. They came here to hang out, enjoy the view. Maybe pick up a couple of cars."

He blinks behind his glasses but says nothing.

"Will this graph of yours help you figure out the odds of Mom being alive or dead?"

I wish I could snatch the words and stuff them back in my mouth. But they're out there now, bouncing around in his brain. He puts down the pencil, takes off his glasses, closes the notebook. The table is still littered with the remnants of breakfast. Clumps of congealed eggs sit on plates, cold, rubbery, and yellow. Dad rights the saltshaker but leaves the granules where they are. On a normal day he wouldn't stand for this. As soon as the meal is over, or there's a spill or whatever, he's in instant clean-up mode. Mom says engineers crave order. He can't help himself.

"We've been over this already," he finally says. "But it's a subject worth revisiting. There's no point in worrying about something outside our sphere of influence. We have to assume she's okay and trying to reach us."

There are many Dad-isms that really get to me, but his Sphere of Influence speech—that's got to be right near the top. It's his logical adult brain torturing my freewheeling, irresponsible teenager brain.

Like yesterday.

Once it looked like the PODs weren't going to attack the houses (yet), I spent the day trying to reach Mom. After a couple of hours Dad said it was a waste of time, they were jamming all the frequencies. It was frustrating. We have electricity and running water, but anything that has to do with communication either flat-out doesn't work or is filled with that alien space spam. But I kept surfing the channels anyway until Dad pulled the plug. "CNN is canceled," is all he said.

Later, after dinner, I asked him why he didn't seem more worried about Mom. That's when I got his fifteen-minute Sphere of Influence speech. Boiled down to one sentence, it goes like this: We can't do anything about her situation, so let's focus on ours.

Now he's plotting his little graph and I have to call it what it is: total BS.

"Dad, the PODs deleted every car, truck, and freaking airplane. We're all stuck in our houses until they decide to delete those, too. They conquered our little planet without breaking a sweat. I'd say they're way beyond our sphere of influence."

"We have the Camry."

He cracks me up. He really does. Our street used to be choked with rusty RVs, broken-down trucks, and old Camaros with bad paint jobs up on blocks. Gone. Dad's VW Rabbit—deleted. All that's left is the oil stain in the driveway. But Mom's car is still in the garage, ready to go. Where are the cruise missiles? The F-16s? The nukes? That's what I want to know.

"So that's your secret weapon? A 1997 Camry with a hundred thirty-two thousand miles and a broken radio?"

He stands up, starts stacking plates. "Josh, if you don't want to count the PODs, fine. I'm not going to make you."

I should help clear the table, but I don't feel like it. I should tell him that I'll count the PODs, but I don't feel like doing that either. So I sit and force myself to look out the window while he crams plates and glasses into the dishwasher. A cat is prowling the back yard, looking for mice. Dutch watches from the patio, too lazy to move. I know exactly how he feels. In the distance a flock of geese head for some unseen pond. This would be an ordinary spring morning except for the alien spaceships floating over the muddy landscape.

And then, as if the day couldn't get any better, Megaphone Man starts up.

The first time we heard him was yesterday afternoon. Right after the PODs' arrival, there were lots of sirens. A half-hour later and that was done. Then people started shouting from their windows, calling out names of people who should be home but weren't, mixed in with the occasional profanity aimed at our uninvited guests. And of course there were guns—it sounded like a war zone for a while. That set off Dutch more than an army of squirrels. Then things quieted down. A resigned silence settled over the neighborhood.

And then it started.

Some guy with a megaphone, calling out, "The Shepherd has returned for His flock! Armageddon is *here*! Repent, all ye sinners, and embrace the Word of the Lord!"

He kept it up for hours. Sometimes he'd mix in Bible verses, sometimes he'd sing parts of a hymn. But most of the time it was the Shepherd Returning message, over and over. People yelled at him to shut up, others said, "Amen." I went to sleep with a pillow over my ears.

And now he's back at it. Megaphone Man.

Dad is wiping down the counter. The table is clear, a gleaming testimony to cleanliness. I ask him, "Do you believe what he's saying?"

Dad says, "When Jesus comes, it won't be in a spaceship."

I say, "Maybe Jesus sent the spaceships."

He stops wiping. Looks at me and says, "Whatever they are, it has nothing to do with God, Jesus, or Armageddon."

Maybe he's right, maybe he isn't. Either way, for the first time in my life I find myself wishing for something I never knew I wanted.

A megaphone.

Then I could express my opinions, see what the neighborhood thinks of that.

DAY 2: LOS ANGELES, CALIFORNIA

- A LONG, DARK SMEAR -

I'm all cried out. I'm still alone. The sky is full of giant spinning black balls that kill anyone stupid enough to go outside. I've been out of the car only twice—once to pee and once to look at the sky. That one look was enough for me. Now I sit alone in the car, staring out the window like a rat in a cage. But I don't have anyone to look at. The parking garage is empty, except for twisted-up cars, broken glass, and the smell of leaking gasoline.

And Speed-Bump Guy.

All I see from here are legs twisted at some crazy angle. I was too afraid to check on him when I left the car. I try not to look over there, but sometimes I do it anyway.

My stomach is growling like an angry dog. I dig up the empty Doritos bags in the back seat. That's good for a few crumbs and a handful of salty jalapeño dust. I'm still insanely hungry, so I lick the insides of the bags. Bad idea. It just makes me thirstier and all the water bottles are empty.

What's driving me nuts is there's a cooler in the trunk with some food and drinks (mostly beer, I think), but I don't know how to get to it. Mom took the keys, and the trunk-release thing inside the car is busted. I know how to break into trunks with a tire iron—I've seen Mom's idiot boyfriend, *ex-boyfriend*, Zack, do it a couple of times. But I don't have a tire iron, and even if I did, it would ruin the trunk and get Mom screaming mad. She said she'd be back, so I'll wait. But for how long? If she's not back by tomorrow morning, then I'm going to break into the other cars and find something to eat. I could go into the hotel, but what's the point? I don't have any money.

In the afternoon two men, a short, thick guy in a blue hooded sweatshirt that says HOOTERS on the front and a tall, bony man with long tattooed arms and a shiny head, argue about what to do with Speed-Bump Guy. The tall man says forget about it. The short man, whose face I can't quite see because of the hood, says throw the carcass outside. They do rock-paper-scissors and the short man wins. They drag the body to the exit, lift him by the arms and legs, swing one-two-three, and heave him into the street. Speed-Bump Guy doesn't touch the ground. There's a flash from the sky and all that's left of him is a dried-up pool of blood and a long, dark smear. After that I'm not hungry.

Day turns into night. I try to sleep. It's hard work with all the cramps and noises and stuff, but I finally do. That lasts two hours, seven minutes, and eight seconds. First it's voices, then flashlights, then smashing windows, then car alarms. It turns into one big ball of noise. I'm afraid to look out the windows, so I curl up in my sleeping bag and wait for it to end. Someone shakes the driver's door while another person pounds on the trunk. They swear and move on. I would have peed myself if I'd had any water to drink. Maybe all they saw was dirt and duct tape and figured there wasn't anything worth taking.

Finally they leave, but I can't get back to sleep. The alarms keep going and going. I know they'll eventually stop, but the sound is driving me crazy. It's like the cars are crying for help. I wrap an old sweatshirt around my head to block out the noise and try to think of something else. Like Mom and her promise. A great big breakfast at Denny's. I'll pick a strawberry waffle with extra whipped cream and lots of butter melting down the sides. I'll pour on so much syrup that the waffle floats. Mom will say, "Would you like some waffle with that syrup?" And if there's enough money maybe I'll even get a chocolate milkshake. Then it's beach time.

I've never been to the beach. Or at least to a beach that's next to an ocean. The stinky mud at Thompson's Pond that people call a beach doesn't count. Mom said the ocean water is cold this time of year but if I wanted to swim I could. She warned me not to open my eyes because the water is salty. There might be jellyfish, too. That's fine with me. All I want to do is jump in the waves like the kids on TV.

Mom and me, strawberry waffles and the beach. Now that's worth waiting for.

- DIRTY LAUNDRY -

Today is Friday. I'm in my bedroom on top of the blankets thinking about all the should-be's. I should be turning in an essay for American Lit and taking a midterm in Chemistry. I should be walking Lynn, my girlfriend for all of two months, to choir practice. She should be asking me to Sadie Hawkins and I should be pretending to think about it before saying yes. And on top of all this, I'm turning sixteen in four days, which means I should be taking the road test for my driver's license in five days. Mom should be coming home from her conference the night before my birthday. We were all going out for pizza and a final practice drive in the Camry. Instead for my birthday present I get an alien invasion. Lucky me.

But there's no guarantee that I'll even live until tomorrow, so why do I care? Now that we're all stuck in our houses, we're pretty much sitting ducks. A knock on my door keeps me from rolling with that depressing thought.

Dad comes into the room. He's holding a pile of crumpled clothes. "Do you have any whites that need to be washed?" he asks. "I'm doing a load."

I say, "The world's about to end and you're doing laundry?"

He says, "I promised Mom I wouldn't let the laundry pile up while she's gone."

I'm looking at the definition of insanity. He's in my room asking for whites. I sit up and point out the window. "Do you think they give a *flying fuck* whether our underwear is clean?"

There, I did it. I dropped the F-bomb. I see it exploding inside his bald head.

After a beat, he says, "I'd prefer it if you didn't swear."

"I swear all the time at school," I say, "just not in front of you."

"Find another way to express your concerns."

Concerns? I'm way past that. "Why?" I ask. "With all the shit that's happening, what does it matter?"

"It disappoints me," he says. "And it would disappoint Mom."

"Then there's a lot about me that will disappoint you."

He walks around my room, picking up various pieces of clothing that I will never wear again, clean or dirty. When he's finished, he walks to the door, stops, and says, "I'm sure we'll have plenty of opportunities to disappoint each other. Let's just try not to start the process too soon." Then he leaves, closing the door softly behind him.

Dinner is ham sandwiches on stale bread with miscellaneous bruised fruits and rubbery vegetables. We dance around serious topics with inane observations, like Dad saying, "Looks like a wind is picking up," and me saying, "I didn't know you put salt on carrots." It's a truce of sorts. Most of the time the only sound is our silverware scraping against the plates while the PODs do their silent dance outside the dining room window. I feed Dutch a couple of hunks of bread off my sandwich. Dad sees this but, amazingly, doesn't say a thing.

After dinner Megaphone Man starts up with his Day of Reckoning announcement. Rather than listen to him, I decide to break the truce and ask Dad a question that is bugging me. I find him in the living room doing a very worthwhile project—folding laundry. The clothes are separated into two piles, his and mine.

"Do you think the PODs are everywhere," I ask, picking up a pair of jeans from my pile and folding it, "or just here?"

"What do you mean by 'just here'?"

"Over the United States."

"Why would you think that?"

"Maybe they're not from space. Maybe we're being invaded by another country."

He's shaking his head. I don't know where this idea came from. It's something I thought up just now, but I'm liking it. If nothing else, it rattles his chain.

"No, really," I say. "Maybe it's the Chinese, or South Korea—"

"*North* Korea."

"Yeah, whatever. One of those communist countries."

Dad looks at me. "What are they teaching you in school these days?"

"I'm serious. What's wrong with my theory?"

He picks up a shirt, shakes it, puts it on the coffee table, smoothes it out. Starts folding one side, then the other. My dad, the folding machine. "This technology is way beyond anything man-made," he says. "Somehow they figured out a way to cancel gravity. And then there are the weapons—the head-exploding screech that targets only humans, the frequency jamming, those beams of light."

"The ones that killed Jamie right outside our door? But before I could help her because *someone* grabbed me from behind. You mean *those* beams?"

This stops the folding machine, but only for a second. "It's alien technology, Josh. Nothing else makes sense."

I drop the subject. He's right and we both know it. I also know he's not finished making his point. I pick up a shirt from my stack and wait. He watches my technique. The folded shirt is uneven and lumpy, not the symmetrical objects of art that he has piled up neatly in front of him. I know he wants to show me the right way to do it. The thought of all those wrinkles is torturing him. Somehow he resists.

Finally he says, "They can't cover the whole planet. There'd have to be millions of them. I think they're just over the major population centers—and strategic sites."

"Then why are they here, over us? We're just some shi— I mean, *crappy* little town."

It's true. We have only one high school. One stupid mall with lame stores that keep closing, one broken-down theater showing movies that came out on video two months ago. There's a paper-processing plant that stinks up our air when the wind blows, a bunch of used-car lots selling overpriced rust buckets, and one crummy bridge spanning a greasy, polluted river with toxic fish. Once you hit the interstate leaving town, all you see is desert and tumbleweed for fifty miles in any direction.

"We're close to a nuclear power plant," he says.

"That's sixty miles away."

"When you travel billions of miles, what's another sixty?"

"Okay then. If you travel billions of miles, you don't make a trip like that unless you plan to stay a while."

He chews on that one in silence. Score one for me.

His folding is done. His stuff is in three stacks: shirts, pants, socks and underwear. The display looks like it should be on a shelf at L.L. Bean. Even the socks are tidy—paired and rolled into little sock balls. He eyes my work but says nothing.

"So how long are they staying, Dad?"

"As long as it takes."

"To do what?" I'm not folding clothes anymore. I'm wadding them up.

"Accomplish their plan."

"And that plan would be?"

His eyes, blue and suddenly watery, lock onto mine. After a moment, he takes one of my fabric balls, a T-shirt, and folds it the right way. He says, "That's the million-dollar question, Josh. Let me know when you figure it out." He carefully combines his stacks and heads for the stairs. "Good luck with the folding."

The dead space he leaves behind fills up with Megaphone Man droning on about the end of the world. I'm sick of Armageddon this and End of Time that. I run to the door, open it, and yell at him to shut the hell up.

I wish the rest of the neighborhood would yell at him, too. But no one's saying anything. I figure they're either too dead or too scared. We're all bugs on a sidewalk, waiting for the boot to fall. But when that finally happens, one thing is for sure.

I'll be wearing clean underwear.

- SOUP AND A SANDWICH -

A man is trying to break into the trunk of the blue sedan next to ours. I think he's a looter because the owner got zapped on the first day. I watch from the shadows of the back seat as he leans into a tool I can't see. It scrapes against metal. I haven't seen him before. He's short and round with thin, curly hair and wire-rimmed glasses that keep sliding down his nose. He looks around, pushes up his glasses, leans again. The tool slips. He swears under his breath. I bet he's never broken into anything other than a refrigerator.

The green door opens. Two men head straight for him, walking fast. One I recognize right away. He's wearing the same Hooters sweatshirt he had on when he tossed Speed-Bump Guy into the street. The hood shades half his face, making the one eye I can see look small and dark. The other man is huge, like a bear, with a thick black beard and long black hair tied in a ponytail. He's a few steps behind Hoodie, his face unreadable behind all that hair, but his eyes are steady on the smaller man in front of him. Of the two, I think Hoodie is the man to watch.

Hoodie yells, "Hey, my friend! You heard the orders—no one allowed in the Forbidden Zone."

Round Guy jumps at the noise. He sees them, stands up, and says, "But...but this is my car."

Hoodie walks up to him. "So you're bustin' into your own trunk?"

Round Guy says, "It's my car. You have no right—"

Hoodie says to Black Beard, "You think this is his car?"

Black Beard says, "Nope." His voice is soft but very deep. More like a rumble from the bottom of his chest.

Hoodie says, "It's a con-sensus then. You look more like a BMW man. No way your ride's a piece-a-crap rental like this."

Round Guy looks at one, then the other. He wipes sweat from his forehead, slides his glasses up.

Hoodie says, "This your car then where's the keys?"

Round Guy says, "My, uh, my wife lost them."

Hoodie, smiling, says, "That a fact? Your wife? In all the chaos and pan-de-monium?"

Round Guy nods. But it's a careful nod, like he's not sure whether to agree or not.

Hoodie says to Black Beard, "You believe him?"

Black Beard says, "Nope."

Hoodie is focused on Round Guy, but Black Beard is scanning the lot. His eyes settle on this car. I freeze, hoping the shadows make me invisible. He lingers a moment, then moves on.

Hoodie says to Round Guy, "Here's the deal, my friend. You describe the con-tents of this trunk. Then we'll open it. If you're right, all we got is the problem of you being where you're not supposed to be. No one gets hurt—at least not *much*. On the other hand..."

There's a soft click. It reminds me of Zack snapping a chicken bone. The curved steel of a switchblade appears in Hoodie's right hand. He spins it twice on his finger like an old-time gunslinger. Then he does some tricky thing where the blade weaves between his fingers, almost like it's alive. After a few seconds he stops, examines the tip, uses it to dig at a fingernail. Black Beard isn't looking around anymore. His attention is on Hoodie, dark eyes glued to that blade.

Round Guy's glistening face is the color of bread dough.

Hoodie says, "On the other hand if you can't describe the *con-tents* of this trunk, which I believe to be the case, well then..."

Hoodie flicks his wrist and the blade disappears. He holds his hands out like a magician who just made a rabbit disappear, smiles slow, and says, "Then we got us a bona fide *sit*-u-ation."

Round Guy gulps like a beached whale. "Look, I don't want any trouble—"

Hoodie says, "Oh, you already *got* trouble, my chubby little friend. The question is what *kind*."

Round Guy slides up his glasses. Licks his lips. His mouth opens but nothing trickles out.

Hoodie says, "See, like maybe you got drugs in there? Some illegal *con*-tra-band?"

Round Guy puts his hands up and out like everything's cool. "Hey, I can do this some other time. I mean I can—"

Hoodie takes a step toward Round Guy, saying, "You can't do this some other time, my friend. Cause there ain't gonna be *another time*."

Hoodie's fist slams into Round Guy's stomach, once. I hear the rush of air leave his lungs. Something metal drops out of Round Guy's hand, clanks on the cement. He sinks to the ground like a balloon deflating. I can't see him now, but I hear the squeaks of him trying to breathe. Black Beard turns to face the green door, his hands clenched into fists.

Hoodie, smiling down on Round Guy, says, "You gotta work your abs, my friend. Otherwise you're gonna have some serious back problems." Then, to Black Beard: "Like punching a feather pillow, man. I think I bruised my knuckles on his spine. Never, ever let your body get that soft."

Black Beard stares at him. He says something to Hoodie, but I can't hear what. I think it's in Spanish.

Hoodie shrugs and says, "Desperate times, desperate measures." He heads for the green door.

Black Beard lifts Round Guy to his feet. His legs are all floppy like they don't have any bone. He slings him over his shoulder like a sack of potatoes and follows Hoodie across the lot. They disappear inside. The green door clicks behind them.

I wait ninety-three seconds.

I slide out of the car. Round Guy's glasses are on the ground. I pick them up, start to put them in my pocket, then decide to leave them where they are. I look for that metal tool. It's under the blue car next to a rear tire—a six-inch flathead screwdriver. Not a tire iron, but it'll do.

It takes me sixteen minutes and lots of prying, but eventually there's a click. The trunk of our car pops open. I'm so thirsty my tongue feels like it's glued to the top of my mouth. I lift out the cooler along with some extra clothes that might come in handy. While I'm doing that I see the clothes Mom wore the night we pulled into LA. They're folded and tucked into a corner next to the spare tire. It's her favorite jeans and the Red Sox sweatshirt I bought her for Mother's Day. My throat gets lumpy. She must have changed into her "interview outfit" in the car while I was sleeping. That was what, a million years ago? The sweatshirt would come in handy against the cold at night, but I think no, when she comes back, she'll need it more than me. That outfit didn't cover much skin.

I lug the cooler back into the car and open it up. There are lots of treasures, but my first move is to twist open the only bottle of water. I drink it so fast it spills out the sides and soaks my T-shirt. Half the bottle is gone before I think maybe I should save some. I cap it, then look at what I've got. Four cans of beer, one can of Mountain Dew, a half-gone package of pepper-jack bologna we stole from a Safeway in Bakersfield, eight soggy hot-dog buns, a handful of mustard packages, and some stinky yellow cheese sealed in a Ziploc bag. There used to be ice, but it's all melted so the mishmash is floating around in a brownish, lumpy glop. It looks like soup to me. I figure the beer will last the longest, so that means it's bologna and cheese and Mountain Dew now. There's an empty water bottle on the floor of the car. I fill it with the soup. Squeeze some mustard on the bologna. Wrap it around a piece of stinky cheese. I'll have a hot-dog bun later. Call it dessert.

Mom would be proud, wherever she is. I fixed lunch all by myself.

DAY 4: PROSSER, WASHINGTON

- TAKING OUT THE TRASH -

I'm having a dream about Mom. She's making her famous oat-bran pancakes and telling me about a game she played as a kid, something about hiding from monsters. As long as she was very, very quiet, she could hide anywhere and the monsters would never catch her. She says now it's time for me to play. I ask her why. She puts a finger to her lips and whispers, "Because they're here," and then she starts counting, one, two, three... I tell her she needs to hide, too, but she doesn't listen. The front door starts shaking, then blows open. An intense blue light fills the entryway. A big shadow writhing like a ball of snakes stretches across the floor. Mom keeps flipping pancakes and counting, ten, eleven, twelve... I scream. All that comes out of my mouth is a cloud of blue vapor.

That's when I wake up. There's a huge wind. It's like an invisible hand pressing against the walls and glass. I hear shingles peeling off the roof. My mind is too full of the dream to let me go back to sleep. I stay in bed and wait for Dad to get up while the hand shakes our house like a toy.

I want to tell Dad about the dream, but I know it would be a mistake. All I'd get would be another Sphere of Influence speech. Even if things were normal I wouldn't tell him. Mom and I, we talk about our dreams all the time. Even though they're random and crazy she still thinks every dream, no matter how stupid, means something. Dad tolerates the discussions, but he never contributes. He says he doesn't dream. How is that possible? I guess that means he doesn't have nightmares, which is a definite bonus these days.

I find him in the kitchen making breakfast. But it's not oat-bran pancakes. We're talking fried eggs in olive oil, which I hate, and bacon, which I love. He's closed the curtains, shutting out the view of the back yard—and, of course, of the PODs. With the curtains closed, the house feels cold and small, but the breakfast smells are good. I sit down, my back to the window. The notebook is open on the table. Today's entry reads: *May 18 / 8:57 a.m. – 120 PODs. Visibility down. Clouds may account for reduced inventory.*

"You hear the coyotes last night?" he asks.

It was bizarre. We occasionally hear coyotes in the distance, but never like that. It sounded like they were yapping right outside my window. Maybe that was part of my dream?

"How could I not? Dutch went nuts. He spent the rest of the night licking his balls."

"Maybe you shouldn't let him sleep in your room."

"Maybe," I say.

He says, "This is the last of the eggs."

"Fine with me."

"You won't be saying that in a couple of weeks."

"Yes, I will. I've been meaning to ask you, how do you make your eggs so rubbery?"

"It's one of life's great mysteries." He slides the greasy pile onto my plate. "I added extra rubber, just for you."

The olive oil gives the eggs a greenish brown color. Vomit comes to mind. He smiles and sits down across from me. It's the first smile I've seen in forty-eight hours. There's one egg and two slices of bacon on his plate. I have three eggs and six slices of bacon.

"Do I really have to eat all this?"

"It's going to spoil if you don't."

"You can have my eggs."

"I'm on a diet."

I stab at an egg. Thick yellow fluid oozes out. For some reason my stomach is churning. Every time I eat something I'm wondering if it's my last meal. I don't want the world to end when I've got a belly full of Dad's oily eggs.

"Josh," he says. "We need to talk about our situation."

Here we go. I put down my fork. "A *situation?* It's an *invasion*, Dad. Call it what it is!" Then I do it again. I drop the F-bomb.

He stares hard at me for a moment. I'm not sure which bothers him more, "invasion" or the swearing. He takes a deep breath and says, "If you feel the urge to use profanity in front of me, please choose a different word."

"A different word. Like what? 'Banana'?"

"I suggest 'freaking.'"

"Freaking?"

"That's my preference." Dad looks at his plate, forks the last of his egg. We're being invaded, life as we know it is about to end, and he's stressing over my vocabulary.

"Okay, then. Back to our little 'situation.' What's your *freaking* point?"

"We've been living high on the hog too long."

"Meaning what?"

"It's time to start rationing food."

He waits for me to say something. I chew on a piece of bacon, wait for the flood.

"All right. First we cook the perishable goods, then the items that taste better heated, like soups and pastas, because we don't know how long the electricity or running water will last. When that goes, we'll cook using the camp stove until we run out of fuel. Then we'll burn furniture until it's gone. Then we eat the canned fruits and vegetables in the pantry, and then it's down to your hoard of potato chips and candy."

"Wow," I say, "someone's been busy making a plan." Dad thumbs through the notebook, looking for something. I slip Dutch a piece of bacon under the table.

Dad finds what he's looking for. He tears it out of the notebook, hands me a piece of paper with a list titled *Survival Priorities*. It's numbered from 1 to 25, the important stuff bulleted and underlined with a red pen. It says things like fill every container with water, including the bathtub, take inventory of all food items and medicines, figure out what we can burn if the power goes out, break down furniture, recharge batteries—even floss our teeth and keep up with my studies. It all sounds reasonable in a post-apocalypse sort of way. At least it's something to do. But there's a couple of issues with the food-rationing plan that bother me.

"What happens when we run out of candy?"

"We reevaluate."

"Reevaluate, huh? What about him?" I ask, nodding to Dutch. His sad eyes watch my every move, hoping for another tasty piece of bacon.

"We have ten pounds of dry dog food left. Normally, that would last about ten days. I had hoped to pick up more food for him this weekend, but obviously that's not happening. We can feed him, or," he says with a pause, "we can eat it ourselves when our food runs out."

"You're saying we should starve Dutch?"

"Dutch is a dog, he'll fend for himself."

"Can people even eat dog food?"

"Dogs eat people food. I'm sure it works both ways."

I look at Dutch. He's a big, fat, lazy yellow Lab with gray whiskers and a bad hip. The only way he'd catch a rabbit is if it jumped into his mouth.

Thinking I'd rather die than take Dutch's food, I say, "Do we have to make that decision right now?"

"There are lots of tough decisions we'll have to make. You need to realize—" Dad starts, then changes his mind. "Okay, let's hold off on that one for a couple of days. But beginning tomorrow, he doesn't get any of our water."

"Where's he going to get it?"

"The creek behind the house."

Our house borders a swamp. Dad calls it a "wetland sanctuary," but it's really an algae-covered stinkhole filled with sludgelike green water and plastic waste. It's closer to a sewer than a creek. When I was younger I used to catch frogs in the reeds bordering the creek, but one year they all floated to the surface, bellies yellow and bloated. There weren't any frogs after that.

Barely able to keep from screaming, I say, "Why don't you just kill him now and—"

There is a loud *pop*, followed quickly by two more. Then nothing.

"Gunshots," Dad says, standing up fast. "From the apartments, I think."

We run to the living room window, just in time to see a door open across the street. Two men hold up a slumping body. It's a big guy, naked and hairy, pale chest and fat stomach streaked with red. They push him out the door. He's standing on the sidewalk, barely. In that moment I recognize him. He yelled at Dutch last summer for peeing on his new truck. Two beats later and there's a flash of light. The guy is gone. A wave of nausea sweeps over me. It's like hauling out the garbage. As long as it's human, they'll take it.

"What was that about?" I say, blinking back the image that was there just seconds ago.

Dad stares at the empty sidewalk. He waits, then says in a voice I barely hear, "So dawn goes down to day, nothing gold can stay."

I know the line. It's from a poem he read to me after my third-grade teacher died in a car accident. I'm not much into poetry, but that one stayed with me.

There's some shouting going on in the apartments. It's too far to make out what they're saying, but I turn my back to the window. It's time to leave. I'm afraid I'll hear that *pop* again.

And even more afraid the door will open.

- MOVING DAY -

The soup is gone. So's the soggy buns. Two pieces of stinky cheese, one slice of bologna, and three glugs of water—that's all I've got left. Oh, and one can of beer. I've been sipping it slow to make it last. So far that isn't a problem. It tastes awful, which makes me wonder how Zack could drink so much. Sometimes when Mom was out working he'd suck down a whole six-pack in the time it took me to finish a soda and a Slim Jim. But anything is better than the soup. I think the soup gave me a bad case of the runs. There's a place behind a little green Toyota that I hope to never see again. But I'm thirsty and the beer makes me want to pee. That means getting out of the car. And that's something I hate to do.

Hoodie keeps coming out here.

Sometimes he's alone, but most times he's not. Day or night, it doesn't matter. They laugh and swear over who gets what. Ever since he punched Round Man I haven't seen anyone else but him and his friends. I figure they're looking for food or maybe drugs or both. There's so many wrecked cars down here that I've been left alone—so far. It's only a matter of time. I want to stay in this car, but if I stay too long Hoodie will find me. That could be a good thing, but I doubt it. Judging by how things are going up to this point, I figure it's best to keep hiding.

And hiding is something I do better than anyone.

The secret is to hide in a place that has already been searched. That's how I always hid from Zack when he was drunk. I'd be in the closet while he was looking under the bed. Then when he turned his back I'd slip under the bed. He never figured it out. I tried telling this to Mom, that we could hide from him in town, but she wouldn't listen. She said we needed to get as far away as possible. We drove from Erie, Pennsylvania, to Los Angeles in three days. We were headed for a friend's house in San Diego, but the radiator blew in Bakersfield, so that wiped out our cash. We made it to LA with no money and the tank on "E." That's why I'm in a parking garage and Mom is interviewing for a job. A job that would last an hour, tops.

It's time to move. I've been watching that SUV, the one I noticed on the first day. The mom with the two kids never came back. The girl's stuffed rabbit is still on the ground where she dropped it. I'm afraid to pick it up because someone might figure out that I'm here. So it just lies on the cold cement and reminds me of that awful day when Mom left with the whispering man. The bald guy with the tattoos already broke into the SUV, so I doubt he'll bother with it. There's a security light close, but not too close, and lots of shadows all around. It looks big, so there should be plenty of room for my sleeping bag and clothes and places to hide if I need them. It's still kind of sideways from when it got rammed, which is good for me. That means I have a perfect view to watch this car.

For when Mom comes back.

My backpack is loaded. It's dark outside and no one has been in the garage for three hours. Sticking to the shadows, I make my way to the SUV. It's a Lincoln Navigator. The big rear window is broken but not smashed. The window on the front passenger side is completely gone. My hand shakes as I reach for the door handle. I've never busted into a car before. It feels like I'm doing something illegal. But that's crazy thinking—nobody is going to yell at me now. The door is unlocked. I slip inside, promising myself that if I take something, even if it's just a crumb, I'll leave a note.

The first thing that hits me is the smell of leather. It reminds me of shopping with Mom one day. We stopped at a furniture store and sat on all the expensive couches—"Just for kicks and giggles," she said. My shirt smelled like leather the rest of the day. I didn't want to wash it.

There's barely enough light from outside to see what I'm doing. The front passenger seat is covered with small diamonds of broken glass. I wrap my hand in my shirtsleeve and sweep them onto the floor. The glove compartment is hanging open, its contents tossed around. I find folded-up maps of California, Nevada, and Oregon, a small notebook with two pages of neat handwritten information about miles traveled and gallons of gas. While I'm flipping through the pages I think I hear something, like a small squeak. I stop and listen. It doesn't happen again, so I keep searching.

The ashtray holds some change and half a stick of gum. I start chewing on the gum but leave the money. The storage bin between the front seats has a stack of four CDs, all country, which I hate, and a power cord for something, probably a cell phone. There is one treasure the looters missed. A pen with a small flashlight that works. I stuff it into my pack.

The compartments in the doors are just as worthless—a hair-brush, some greasy food wrappers, and a remote for a garage door opener. Zack always hides stuff under the seats, so I check there. Nothing under the passenger side except pieces of glass and one pencil that could be useful. But under the driver's seat—that's where I find something interesting.

It's a black metal box a little bigger than Zack's briefcase. There's a drawer on the front with a silver keyhole. The drawer is locked. I yank on the box. It doesn't budge. I try to pry the drawer open with my pencil, but all I do is break the lead. Whatever is in the box must be important, probably tools and maybe some cash. But that will have to wait until later. I need to get moved in.

I search the rest of the SUV. It's huge compared to Mom's Nova. There are two seats in back, one with a booster that has smears of something dark on the cushion and seatbelt. It's either chocolate or dried blood. I remember the girl's head was bleeding after the crash so I'm pretty sure it's not chocolate. The family must have been on a road trip because there are coloring books full of pictures of unicorns, three Spiderman comics, and a shoebox crammed with baseball cards. I roll up the comics—they go in the pack. The storage compartment between the seats is full of cray-ons. I stick my fingers in the cracks between the armrests and get lucky—twenty Skittles, my favorite candy.

This car is so gimongous there's even a row of seats behind the back seats. It's comfy, like my favorite couch in the expensive furniture store, with plenty of room to stretch out. Perfect for a sleeping bag and my backpack. There's a rear compartment that I can get into by folding down the seats, but I decide to explore that in the morning when the light is better. I could use the flashlight pen, but why waste the batteries? I roll out my sleeping bag, crawl inside, and use the backpack for a pillow. There's a kind of nasty smell back here—I'm not sure what the problem is, but it can't be much worse than the shirt I'm wearing.

I close my eyes and wait for sleep. Hopefully it will come without bringing pictures of Speed-Bump Guy bouncing under the cars. I hate it when that happens. My stomach growls, which reminds me I didn't have dinner. That's easy to fix. One bite of bologna. One nibble of cheese. A sip of beer. There, dinner is done. I close my eyes again. The silence and the dark surround me.

But not for long. There it is again—that squeak.

It's definitely coming from inside the car, and close. I hold my breath and wait. I hear it—the back compartment. I scramble out of my sleeping bag and fold down one of the seats. The smell is so bad my eyes water. But the sound is louder. I know what it has to be. My heart pounds as I fumble in my pack for the flashlight pen. I find it, switch it on, aim the small beam into the shadows.

It's a kitten in a small wire cage.

The cage is on its side with a pink towel covering the bottom edge. I open the door and lift her out. She's the size of a fuzzy softball, big gray eyes ringed with dried goop, yellow hair the same color as mine. She smells like cat pee. There are two empty dishes in her cage. One has *Cassie* written with red crayon on the side. I think back to the first day, when the boy tried to run to the SUV but his mother wouldn't let him. He screamed like he forgot something important. Now I know what that something was.

"Hello, Cassie," I say.

The sound startles me. It's the first words I've spoken since

Mom left. It must have startled Cassie too because she starts mewing like crazy. An alarm goes off in my brain, but I don't care. I hold her close to my chest and stroke her fur. She settles down.

"Let's get you cleaned up," I whisper. "You stink worse than me."

I carry her back to my couch bed, spill a few drops of water on the towel, and wipe her down. Then I give her a couple of sips of my beer. She laps it up and looks around for more.

I say, "Guess that means you're hungry, too."

I tear off a sliver of bologna. She gobbles it down like it was a piece of steak.

The alarm goes off in my head again. As much as I'd like to keep her, I have to be smart. Like Mom would say, who needs another mouth to feed? I give her one more sip of beer. I promise to let her go first thing tomorrow. Right now she needs some company.

"You're a very lucky kitty," I whisper.

We burrow into the warmth of my sleeping bag. Beneath it all I hear the buzz of the security light. For a moment I wonder how dark it would be without the lights. No darker than my closet at home, that's for sure.

Then Cassie starts to purr. For once I'm not thinking about Hoodie with his knife, the aliens, or the long, dark smear. Or even Mom. Cassie feels good against my skin.

That's what I'm thinking when I fall asleep.

- CLICK -

It's official. The man is crazy.

First the laundry, now this. We're filling containers with water. Jugs, mugs, bottles, and cans are lined up in neat rows on the kitchen counter. He's upstairs filling the bathtub. I'm in the kitchen, filling—I can't believe this—Ziploc freezer bags. They look like supersized versions of those cheesy prizes you win on the midways at county fairs, only without the goldfish that die three days later.

This storm of insanity was triggered this morning when the power went off. It stayed off for about fifteen minutes, then came back on. By that time Dad had already mobilized the water brigade. I tried reasoning with him, that it was total overkill, but he didn't buy my argument.

I said, "Haven't you been listening? It's the End of Days."

He said, "It's the end of us wasting our resources."

I said, "But Megaphone Man says we should embrace the Lord and go to the light."

He said, "Embrace this," and handed me the box of Ziplocs. "If you think of anything else to fill, fill it." I thought of something, but decided not to say it.

So here I am, sealing little plastic bags. Fortunately the box had only ten left. I'm thinking they'd make excellent ammunition for when the alien storm troopers knock down the door. Actually, they'd probably melt the door—but anyway, we can peg them with these water balloons! Then Dutch will gnaw on their tentacles while Dad finishes them off with his Sphere of Influence speech. Bada-boom, invasion over. End of story.

The box is empty and there's no more room on the counter. That means there's no point in thinking of things to fill. I hear the water running upstairs, which means Dad is still occupied. Now is a good time to snag a snack. I go to the pantry. The only choice is an opened box of graham crackers. Not my first choice, but it'll do. I crash on the slouch couch in front of the unplugged television, pick up the remote, and pretend I'm surfing channels.

CNN: Death and destruction. *Click.*

ESPN: Balding ex-jocks yakking about steroids. *Click.*

FOX News: Talking heads arguing about global warming. *Click.*

CSPAN: *Click.*

MTV: Lame reality show. *Click.*

NBC: A lady singing about an odorless air freshener. *Click.*

FOX: *The Simpsons.* It's the episode where the whole family goes into the witness-protection program. Homer is being grilled by two FBI agents.

I take a bite of a graham cracker and watch. It would be so much better if I had some peanut butter to spread on the crackers, but tragically we ran out yesterday. The jar is full of water now. I yawn. This episode is a classic, but I've seen it three hundred times.

Click.

I put down the remote. As usual, there's nothing on that's worth my time.

I crunch on another peanut-butterless cracker. It's a sign of things to come. Seems this was a bad time for an invasion. Dad was waiting for Mom to come home before going to the grocery store to stock up the pantry. So there's all this stuff we should have that we don't. Like peanut butter. And dog food. And frozen pizzas. And Cheese Nips. And Dr. Pepper. And bottled water. And those amazing granola bars with the chocolate bottom and caramel top and Rice Krispies in between. Alex and I once polished off two boxes of those babies while we watched *Die Hard 1* for the third consecutive time. Mom and Dad were at a play or a movie or something. We both agreed it was the best dinner ever.

Alex.

I can't believe this is the first time I've thought of him. He's only been my best friend since a month after my family moved to this hamlet six years ago. That's the word that Alex uses to describe our little town. It's the smallest, most medieval title he could think of. It also works because there's a diner on Wine Country Road that sells five mini-burgers, or hamlets, for a buck fifty. We eat there at least twice a week during lunch hour.

Is he still alive? I think so. He usually takes the bus to school, or gets a ride from us, so chances are he's stuck in his house like we are in ours. His dad might not be, though. He's one of those crazy early-morning-jogger types. I've always thought jogging at five a.m. was a dumb-ass thing to do. Now I know why.

Alex is lucky. He lives in a duplex next to the apartment building across the street. Which means there's a POD right over his house. Which means he's lucky because he can't see it. I, on the other hand, am not lucky. I see it every time I look out the living room window. That, and a crashed bicycle surrounded by rolled-up newspapers.

Alex is the one who dared me to ask Lynn out. He spent two weeks convincing me that my odds were better than fifty-fifty. He's also the one who saw me through my dark days, when I knew in my soul that the only way to express my creative self was to tattoo a spider on my neck descending from my left ear, paint my lips black, and pierce both eyebrows. He said some people can do Goth or punk or whatever and make it work. Like Marilyn Manson. And Brittney what's-her-name from homeroom. "You," he said, laughing, "you'd just look stupid."

Dutch is sitting in front of me watching graham crackers disappear into my mouth. Drool is forming at the corner of his jowls. A slick string drips to the floor. He's studying each move as though I'm eating some amazing food. It's only a stupid cracker. He licks his nose, something he does when he's begging for treats. It's one of his two disgusting habits. The other is, at night he spends hours licking his balls like they're hairy popsicles. The guilt is killing me. I toss him the last graham cracker. His jaws snap and it's gone.

"I can't believe you just did that."

I almost jump out of my skin. "Jesus, Dad! When there's aliens outside, you don't freakin' sneak up on people!"

"And you don't give our food to the dog."

"I'm sorry. I only did it once."

He's leaning against the wall, surveying the room. His eyes zero in on the empty box of graham crackers on the coffee table. "You ate the whole box?"

"I *finished* the box. There was like half a cube left."

"Our food has to last, Josh."

"I know that."

"Do you think I enjoy filling baggies with water?"

"I said I'm sorry!"

He looks at me like I'm this hopeless case. He thinks I don't take the food thing seriously, but I do. It's just we come at it from different angles. His opinion: We should start rationing. Eat less, make it last longer. My opinion: We're going to die any second, so why not live it up? Why starve? The way I see it, the more we eat, the less we leave behind for the storm troopers.

He says, "I think the dog should go back to sleeping outside."

Now Dutch is "the dog." Unbelievable. "Why? It's not like I'm sneaking him steaks while you're asleep."

"You fed him some of your bacon."

I blink but say nothing. This is way beyond creepy.

"He needs to get used to fending for himself."

"Fend for himself? Like he's going to catch a squirrel or something?"

Dad shakes his head. "Just do it. I'm tired of talking about this."

He leaves. I pick up the remote and point it to where he had been standing two seconds ago.

Click.

- BLOATER -

I rip the last piece of bologna into three pieces. Two for me, one for Cassie.

"You better like your breakfast," I say, "because after this it's mice for you."

While she eats, I plan out my day. The first part of the morning was wasted searching for the key to that metal box under the driver's seat. I've been searching all the nooks and crannies for two days and it's no use. The mother must have the key. Whatever is in there doesn't matter anymore. Now it's time to get back to the important stuff.

First, find a new home for Cassie. Second, find more food and water for me. My stomach is growling all the time. Both things mean it's time to do some exploring.

But that could be a problem. If I leave the car and Mom comes back, she may think I'm dead. She'll leave without ever seeing me. I could put a note on the windshield, but if Hoodie finds it first, he'll know I'm here. That could get me punched in the stomach, too.

I ask Cassie, "What do you think I should do? Leave a note or take my chances?"

She looks up at me, then goes back to her piece of bologna.

"What's that? You think I should leave a note?"

Then I think of another thing. If I leave a note and Mom sees it, she'll wait for me. But then if Hoodie finds her before I do—I don't want to think about that.

It's final. No note.

"I'm going to find you a new home," I say. "But you need to be careful. Don't trust anyone. Even if they're nice on the outside. You think they're your friend, then they gobble you up."

Cassie is done. She licks her face with her small pink tongue and looks around as if there should be more. I make a cup out of my hand and pour in a little water. She laps it up, then licks my hand.

"I know what you need," I say, scratching behind her ears. "You need milk." Cassie rolls over. She starts batting at my hand with her tiny claws. Now she's in the mood to play. I give in for about a minute, but then it's time to move on to more important things.

I put on my backpack in case I find some food, pick up Cassie, and tuck her under my arm. We head for the ramp leading up to Level 2. Before we round the corner I glance back at the Nova. I get this terrible feeling I'm making a huge mistake.

I should have left a note.

Level 2 is as bad as Level 1. There's a line of wrecked cars. I count fifteen. Some cars never made it out of their parking spots. All the cars, whether wrecked or not, have smashed windows. I decide this is no place for Cassie. I head up to Level 3.

Not as many cars here. I figure this is about as far as I should go. Cassie starts to mew and I don't know why, so I walk over to a car and put her on the hood. She sits there blinking at me like I can read her mind. But at least she's quiet. I look through the broken window to see what's left. Not much. Pieces of paper, an empty Starbucks cup, glass everywhere. I open the door and look around and under the seats. This person must have liked McDonald's. I find eight French fries wedged between seats and five small plastic tubes of ketchup in a sandwich baggie. I eat the French fries the second I find them. Cold and stiff, but the salt tastes good. I decide to save the packages of ketchup in case I find something to eat that's so disgusting I need some flavor to help choke it down. That's the way it worked at my house whenever Mom cooked liver.

Cassie starts to mew again. It's actually pretty loud, which is the last thing I need. She's like a little siren announcing, *Here we are! Here we are!* I could put her in the car and shut the door, but that feels mean.

"All right," I say in an almost-whisper. "I get it. You're hungry. Well, guess what? So am I. But you don't have to blab it to everyone in the garage." I look around at all the empty cars. "Okay, so no one's here now, but that could change." That just stirs her up even more.

The ketchup gives me an idea. I pick her up, open the door, brush off the glass, and put her on the passenger seat. Then I tear open one of the tubes and squeeze it onto the beige fabric right in front of her. The color reminds me of the blood I saw on the headrest in the SUV.

"What are you waiting for?" I say.

Amazingly, Cassie sniffs it, looks back at me, then starts licking. She must be *really* hungry. I close the door and back away. Now I can search the cars in peace.

I start working my way through the smashed-up line. Each car has a story to tell. The first one belongs to a woman who likes to cook. There are plastic purple and yellow flowers on the dashboard and at least fifty recipes for cupcakes typed on green three-by-five cards wrapped together with a rubber band. I leave the recipes— all they do is make me hungrier—but I keep the rubber band. She must also have a kid, probably a boy, because there is a small red duffel in the back seat with two pairs of underwear, some rolled-up socks, and a pair of camo pants. The pants are a little big, but who cares? I figure all those pockets might come in handy. I make a trade—the pants for my sweats. Pink—he'll like that, I'm sure.

Next up is a blue Toyota pickup truck with a smashed front end. I figure it's owned by a tall, nervous man with a hot girlfriend. The driver's seat is way back, the ashtray is full of cigarette butts without any lipstick, and there's a greeting card with a black-and-white picture on the front of a woman with too much makeup and huge boobs. She's wearing a bikini and standing next to an elephant and talking on a cell phone. The printed message on the inside of the card says: **Don't forget!** The handwriting underneath, all slanty and pretty, says: *to call me when you get to the hotel—947-0120. Can't wait, Jen.* The card still smells like perfume. I find sixteen kernels of cheesy popcorn and half a stick of peppermint gum in the armrest. They go into the plastic bag.

The next car is a VW Jetta with four passenger windows, three tinted and one smashed. The trunk is crushed like an empty beer can. I figure Nervous Guy did it. The license plate fell on the ground. It reads: 150IQ. A bumper sticker on the broken rear window says: *Obey gravity—it's the law.* I'm guessing a college student, probably a guy.

I'm wrong.

There's a body inside. It's an old woman in the back seat. She's still wearing the seatbelt. Her hair is silver, short and curly like a poodle's. At first I think she's alive because her eyes are open, but it takes all of two seconds to figure out she isn't. There's a thick line of dried blood coming from her left ear. Her face is grayish white and puffy. Her mouth is open just a crack, showing the tip of a gray tongue. Her eyes are wide with a glassy stare like a department-store mannequin.

The smell hits me.

Like at the river on a hot summer day when you find a dead fish washed up between the rocks. I don't know why I didn't smell it first thing. I'd be throwing up if I had more in my stomach than six French fries.

I turn to leave, but then I notice something that stops me. She's wearing one of those old-lady dresses, the long, boxy kind with a flowery print and pockets big enough to hold a football. One of the pockets has a rounded lump in it; I'm guessing it's a water bottle. I reach in through the window and open the driver's door. I hold my breath, step into the car, climb back between the seats. Her left arm is blocking the pocket. There's no choice—I have to move it. I take a quick breath, touch her hand. It's cold. The nails are red and long, her fingers curled as if she's holding an invisible glass. The skin doesn't feel right, almost rubbery like a doll's. The muscles are stiff, which surprises me. My stomach lurches. I slowly lift her hand and put in on her lap. I take another breath and reach into her pocket. I pull out the bottle of water, nearly full. I reach in again. A Nestlé candy bar, half eaten. I reach in one more time. A crossword puzzle book about soap operas with a pen clipped to the cover.

I stuff the water, the candy, and the pen into my pockets. Already I'm feeling good about my trade. I leave the book. Then I wonder, how will she finish the puzzles without her pen? It's stupid, I know, but I put it back.

A voice tells me I should close her eyes. I've seen it done on television, so I reach out—but I just can't do it. My brain won't let me touch her cold skin one more time. I leave her eyes open to stare at the spot of blood on the back of the beige headrest.

"Thanks for the water," I say, and crawl out of the car.

I should move on to the next car, but my whole body is shaking. I feel like that smell is clinging to my skin. I need to get away. It's time to go back to my sleeping bag on Level 1. Maybe Mom is waiting for me.

Or maybe someone else. Someone with a knife.

I check on Cassie. She's curled up on the seat, sleeping. I know I have to do it, so I might as well do it now. I quietly squeeze another tube of ketchup on the seat and leave the door open a crack so she's able to get out.

I start walking. It feels good to be moving away from those glassy eyes, that smell. But I get only to Level 2 before I have to stop. My eyes are leaking so bad I can hardly see. I can't afford to lose this much water. That same voice, the one from the car, is telling me Cassie will wake up and she'll be alone. She's too small and scared to take care of herself. And what if Hoodie finds her? I'll let her go when she gets a little older. So I turn around. There's enough food and water in this garage for both of us.

I just have to go out and find it.

- FULL TANK OF GAS -

Dinner is done.

The smell of canned chili, burned as usual, hovers in the air. The dishes are clean and stacked. The counter is wiped down with antibacterial soap, not a crumb or germ to be seen. Dad is in the kitchen doing food inventory, checking off each item on his three-page list. It's something he does twice a day now that he knows his son is a graham-cracker felon. Between this and charting space-ships and folding laundry, I'm amazed he has time to sleep.

I lift the keys to the Camry off the hook in the hall and sneak into the garage. I sit in the car, slide the seat back about six inches, put the keys in the ignition. I turn the ignition to the point where the accessories turn on. The dashboard lights up, red and white. The gauges settle into the appropriate positions. I smile. There's a full tank of gas. I reach up to press the button for the garage door opener, but then I realize that would make too much noise. Dad would hear it for sure. I slip out of the car, pull a lever that disengages the opener, and slowly lift the door until there's enough clearance to back out the car. It's dark outside, so I can't see the local POD, but I know it's there. That's good enough for me.

I get back into the Camry, put on the seatbelt to keep it from beeping, check the rearview mirror, slide the gear shift into reverse, push in the clutch. This is the point where Dad should come running. He should have heard me by now and be yelling at me to get out of the car. But he's too busy counting cans of tomato paste and jars of pickled artichoke hearts. I put my hand on the key, ready to twist—and I sit there.

The car smells like Mom. I breathe her in, the unmistakable scent of flowers that trails behind her when she walks past me in the hall. Her yoga mat is rolled up in the back seat. There's a Starbucks gift card and a Target gift certificate in the storage bin, both gifts I gave her for Mother's Day. There's a yellow sticky note she put on the visor reminding herself to make reservations for the pizza party. I close my eyes. It would take all of five seconds for me to disappear. It would take Dad hours, maybe days, to figure out that I'm gone.

Then the details hit me. Like, what would Dad do? Would he walk out the door or stay in the house and starve? What would happen to Dutch? What if this, what if that? All these details are making me tired. I'm not in the mood for this train of thought. I lift my foot off the clutch, pull the keys out of the ignition. I close the garage door, sneak back into the house, and put the keys on the hook.

Dad must have heard something because he calls me to come see what he found. He's sitting on the kitchen floor with a pile of red-and-white packages piled up at his feet.

"Good news, Josh," he says, holding up a prize. "Twenty-four envelopes of dried milk."

"That's amazing, Dad," I say. I turn around and head for my room. He says something about pancakes in the morning, but I'm not listening. I'm thinking that it isn't the PODs and their death rays. It isn't the empty refrigerator, or the soon-to-be-starving dog, or the baggies full of water on the kitchen counter.

It's knowing that today is my birthday, Mom isn't here, and I can't check my freaking email.

That's what's killing me.

- HACKER -

A slamming sound wakes me.

I peer out. Two men are in the garage. My heart skips a beat. One is Hoodie, his face still dark as usual in the shadow of his hood. The other is the tall thin man with the tattoos and shiny head. He helped Hoodie get rid of Speed-Bump Guy. I saw him again the third day smashing windows with a big hammer. He wasn't even searching the cars, just smashing windows. Back then he was wearing a tank top that showed off the tattoos on his arms. Now he's wearing a collared blue shirt with long sleeves. It could be a uniform.

They're standing under the light by the green exit door. Hoodie has a flashlight in one hand and a big hammer in the other. He shines the beam slowly around the garage. It moves to this end and stops. He points with the hammer. The tall guy nods and coughs. It's rough and throaty, like he's going to hack up a lung. When he's done he reaches into his shirt pocket, pulls out a cigarette, and lights it.

They weave through the maze of cars, talking and laughing. Hoodie swings the hammer, slamming it into taillights as he goes. The noise echoes around me, waking Cassie. She lets out a soft mew. I press her against my shirt. One more peep from her and in the sleeping bag she goes.

They're close enough now for me to hear every word.

The bald man stops, hacks up something, and spits it out. Hoodie shakes his head and frowns. They start walking again. It's hard to tell where they're headed. I figure it's one of the cars closer to the exit. They aren't as banged up as the SUV.

Hacker says, "So Richie, you gonna tell me what we're lookin' for?"

Hoodie has a name. Richie.

Richie says, "Guess."

"It's not money."

A short laugh. "You got that right."

"Drugs?"

Richie pounds another taillight. The next car is the Nova. He says, "Drugs would be sweet, but no. Think about it. With the guests being so restless and all, what's the most valuable commodity given our current sit-uation?"

"You ask me it's smokes, man. A carton of Lucky Strikes would make my week."

Richie's at the Nova. He smashes one taillight, then the other. I feel each blow as if the hammer is hitting me.

He kicks at the broken glass. "I hate Novas. Knew a guy that had one. Sucked oil like a Slurpee. Couldn't sell it so he set it on fire and walked away."

Hacker says, "So it's not money or drugs. Why did Mr. Hendricks send us out here at dark-thirty when we should be sleeping?"

Richie stops and looks at him. For a second I think he's going to club Hacker with the hammer. Then he says, "Guns, you bald-headed dumb-ass. The Holy Grail!"

Hacker says, "But we found 'em all. Three pistols and a shotgun. That's it."

Richie says, "This is America, my friend. A garage this size—we should've filled a U-haul by now."

A flashlight beam stabs through the window. Shadows chase each other across the door and roof. Quiet, like an otter into a river, I slide down to the floor space behind the back seat and curl into a ball. Cassie mews in protest. Her tiny claws rake against my ankles. I resist the urge to bury my head in the sleeping bag. I need to hear what they're saying.

Hacker says, "I done the Navigator already. I'm positive there ain't no gun."

Richie says, "And I've got information *con*-tradicting that statement."

The Navigator! A gun! My brain races—where?

Hacker says, "Like what?"

Richie says, "The lady that owns the Navigator needed asthma spray for her boy. She compensated Mr. Hendricks by telling him about a gun her husband stashes in the car."

"Where's it at?"

"In a safe under the driver's seat."

I picture the black metal box just two rows away from my head.

"A safe, huh? She give you the combination?"

"It needs a key. Says he hides a spare somewhere up front."

"What if her information is wrong?"

"There's gonna be an instant shortage of asthma medication."

They laugh. Hacker goes into another coughing spasm. He's so close I smell the smoke from his cigarette. He spits—it thuds like a meatball hitting the car. A flashlight beam scans the inside of the SUV. I duck my head into the sleeping bag but leave enough of a hole so I can hear. I'm hoping all they see is a pile of rags. The handle lifts on the front passenger door. It opens.

Richie says, "You broke this window, right?"

"Third day. Gotta love bustin' up a Navigator."

"You wipe the glass off the seat?"

"Why would I do that?"

"Well, it's all on the floor now."

The door slams closed.

I nudge Cassie with my foot. She moves, just barely.

Footsteps crunching toward the back. The rear passenger door opens.

Richie says, "You see all this crap? Comic books, a pile of clothes, looks like a sleeping bag on the floor?"

"Man, I boosted so many cars I don't remember."

"What do you remember?"

"A kitten in a cage."

"A what?"

"A kitten in back. Scrawny little thing. Smelled like pee."

"You left it?"

"I'm allergic to cats."

Richie says, "That's gen-u-ine sick, my friend. And you say I'm the mean one?"

The door slams shut. More footsteps. Now Richie says, "There's a cage but no kitten. If I didn't know better I'd say someone has built a little nest."

Richie grunts. I figure he's squeezing through the space between the SUV and the car it smashed into. Footsteps on my side of the car now. They move all the way to the driver's door and stop.

There's another sound. A voice yelling in the distance.

Richie says, "What's he want?"

"He says the water's off."

"How's that my problem?"

"Don't know. But he wants us *now*."

Richie says, "Yeah, well, I'm busy."

The driver's door opens. The SUV drops an inch. My heart pounds so hard my head hurts. My lungs are screaming for air, which makes me wonder about Cassie. If I can barely breathe, what about her? I want to poke her with my toe, but I don't. Richie, his voice at floor level, says, "Bingo!" The SUV shakes. Shakes again, harder. Richie swears. He yells, "It's locked!"

"Can you take the safe?"

"No. It's welded it to the floor." A pause. I hear the click of his knife. Just that one sound makes my stomach clench like a fist. He says, "You going to stand there like an idiot, or help me find a key?"

The passenger door opens. They start tossing things around. The noise is like a hurricane. CD cases snapping, carpet ripping, coins dumped to the floor.

Then Hacker says, "Hey! What the—"

There's a thud. He groans. I think he hit ground.

A new voice, deep, like rumbling thunder, says, "Go back to the hotel."

That can be only one person.

Black Beard.

The SUV rises. Richie says, "What's got your panties all in a bunch?"

Black Beard says, "Mr. Hendricks wants the men and women separated."

"That a fact? Who goes where?"

"Men go to the tenth floor."

Richie says, "Divide and conquer. So much for one big happy family."

Silence.

"Do I get to super-vise the ladies?"

Silence.

"I'm sorry. Does this bother you?" I hear the click of his knife. "There, you feel better now?"

Silence.

Richie says, "You know, my friend, you should work on your attitude. Try to com-*mu*-nicate more. You'll never be voted Security Guard of the Month the way you're going."

Silence.

Richie says, under his breath, "Always one damn crisis after another." The door slams. Footsteps walk fast around the SUV. They fade into the distance.

I count two minutes. That's all I can take. I jab my head out of the sleeping bag and take great gulps of sweet, cool air. I listen. Nothing but the buzz of the security light. I climb onto the seat, reach down to the bottom of the bag. There's a warm ball of fur. It moves, then mews softly.

"Cassie!" I whisper, lifting her out and holding her to my chest. Her purring engine is already starting to fire. "That was a close one. We should be more careful."

I don't know how long they'll be gone, so it's time to act fast. I need to find that key. I've never fired a gun, but Zack let me hold his a couple of times. I think I can figure it out. Cassie curls up on the seat. I crawl up front and start looking.

It's worse up here than it sounded. The window visors are snapped off and cut to shreds. The roof liner is slashed, and the radio is hanging by a wire. Even the door panels are pulled away from the frame. They did all this in less than a minute. I try to think of places they didn't look, but it's hard to imagine where. I use the flashlight pen to look behind and under things, but it feels like a waste of time and batteries. I'm about to switch off my light when I spot the black liner to the ashtray. It's upside down next to the gas pedal. There's a small bump on the side where it should be smooth. I pick it up. A strip of black tape is covering something. I peel back the tape and smile.

A silver key.

I glance over my shoulder at the green door. It's closed and quiet, but who knows for how long. It's almost midnight. Maybe they'll decide to get some sleep before coming back. And maybe they won't. I look under the driver's seat, slide the key in the lock. It turns. I pull out the drawer. It's padded with a thin layer of black foam. There's a thick wad of folded-up fifties wrapped with a rubber band. A cell phone. And a black metal box. It's like a mini-briefcase with a handle and a combination lock with four numbered dials. I lift it out of the drawer. It's definitely big enough to hold a gun, and heavy enough, too. I leave the money and the phone but keep the briefcase. I close the drawer and start to lock it, but my brain flashes a picture of Richie smashing the taillights on the Nova. Mom will have to get that fixed and we don't have any money. There goes our breakfast at Denny's. That gives me an idea. It's stupid, but I can't stop. I find a piece of paper and use the flashlight pen to write a short note:

Guess what I've got.
Bang. Bang.

I slide the note under the money, close the drawer, and put the key in my pocket.

There's some noise coming from behind the green door. Something is happening inside the hotel. The sound is muffled, but I think it's screaming. I climb back to Cassie, carrying the black briefcase in my hand.

I pick her up. She's warm and floppy from sleeping on my bag. Her eyes open.

"Look what I found," I say, showing her my prize. "The Holy Grail."

DAY 9: PROSSER, WASHINGTON

- CONTACT -

I'm watching the apartments across the street. I do this for hours, binoculars glued to my eyes while I sit in the comfy red chair I dragged over to face the living room window. It's a fascination of mine ever since the gunshot episode. Not because I'm a sicko freak hoping to catch a murder in progress. I do it because it keeps my mind off the alternatives. I tell Dad I'm looking for changes in the POD. I even have a notebook that I use to write down bogus observations, like: *2:17pm – Subject slightly changed color or Subject moved five centameters to left, then fired blaster beam at old lady with red hat.* Dad looks at the notepad from time to time. His only comment so far: "Centimeter is spelled with an i."

I have a system. I start at the window on the bottom right and move across each floor until I reach the upper-left apartment on the third story. Some windows have curtains, some don't. One lap takes me about fifteen minutes unless something interesting is going on, and that happened only once, not including the naked fat guy with the bullet holes. I saw a woman dancing in a white dress. She kept passing in front of the window, twirling and spinning, sometimes really shaking it up. I liked how she'd toss her head back and laugh, her long blond hair dangling down behind her, then flying out when she did one of her spins. I keep checking back, but there's a curtain over the window now. Even if I never see her again, I'd say my time here is well spent.

I hear Dad moving around behind me. I put down the binoculars, check my watch, pick up the pad, and write: *4:38pm POD reverses rotation and nearly crashes.*

I pick up the binoculars and resume the search. The window on the second floor, three over from the right—it's cracked and missing a shutter. Five years ago this apartment building was new and attractive with fresh white paint and green doors with matching shutters. Now it's a dull brown, the grass in front is mostly weeds, and there's usually some kind of trash out front blowing around in the wind. Moving to the right—nothing, nothing, then the old lady with the paisley scarves. She used to sweep the sidewalk in front of her door every morning. She's married to the French guy—Henri— who fixed my bike last spring for twenty bucks. I think she's watering a plant. She turns and walks away. I move on.

Third floor now, scanning left to right. It looks like a total bust—and *bam!*

She's standing at the window looking through a pair of binoculars. I recognize her from the bus stop. Short blond hair, yellow backpack, wire-rimmed glasses. She was always off in her own world, her face buried in a book. I think she's a freshman. I don't know her name, but I think it's Amanda or Aimee or something like that. There's this unspoken rule at the bus stop—the apartment kids form one group, the house kids form another.

I think she's looking at me. I raise my hand and wave. She waves back. She reaches down for something—a piece of paper. She starts writing, her hand moving in big sweeping arcs. Then she turns her head like someone said something to her—and she's gone.

Two seconds later a tall, skinny dude with a patchy beard and no shirt looks out the window. He's in his twenties, maybe early thirties. Definitely too young to be her father. I've seen him around the neighborhood once or twice. I think he drives an old pickup with a dirt bike in the back. He opens the window, spits, closes it, and walks away.

I wait for a few minutes. She doesn't come back.

I put the binoculars on the windowsill and rub my eyes. My head hurts and I wonder why. Maybe it's because I'm smiling. For a moment I had communication with another human being, one who isn't obsessed with folding laundry.

DAY 9: LOS ANGELES, CALIFORNIA

- DUST, DENTS, AND DUCT TAPE -

I put the gun case on the seat and take a deep breath. What should I do? Keep trying to open it to see if there really is a gun inside, or move to another car and *then* worry about the gun? The metal is thick—I tried prying it open with the screwdriver, but that didn't work. Same thing for picking the lock.

I glance at Cassie, hoping for some amazing words of wisdom. She looks up at me with big kitten eyes. Hungry eyes, I'm sure.

"Yeah," I say, "you think I should move first, then get some food, then worry about the case." That seems like a good plan. Richie is coming back, and I don't want to be here when he does. A part of me wants to hide close by so I can see his face when he opens the drawer, but that would be stupider than leaving the note in the first place.

"You are a smart kitty," I say. "It's time to find us a new home."

A flash of pain burns my heart. I remember Mom saying those exact words—*find us a new home*. It was only what, last week? But it feels like last year. I came home from school and her car was in the driveway. A little alarm started ringing in my head. She usually didn't get off work until after supper. I looked through the windows. The red plastic cooler was on the floor in back, and on the back seat there was a pile of clothes, mine and hers, along with a grocery bag full of snacks. The front passenger seat had two pillows and a stack of maps.

Mom was waiting for me when I walked into the house. The living room was thick with cigarette smoke. Her eyes were red and moist and her makeup was smeared. But whatever made her cry had turned into something else. Something hard. "It's time to find us a new home," she said, her voice steady. She told me I had fifteen minutes to pack the suitcase on my bed—then we were leaving. "Only bring the stuff you really need," she said. "Don't ask questions, there'll be time for that later. And don't stand there with your mouth hanging open. Just do it!"

I went into my room not sure what to think. We were running from Zack, that much I knew. But where to, and why now? The suitcase was on my bed, open and waiting. I looked around trying to figure out where to start, what parts of my life to keep and what parts to leave behind. Mom yelled, "Three minutes!" My mind was spinning, my hands shaking. *Be calm*, I told myself. *Think!* My sketching notebooks, keep. Stuffed koala from Zack, leave. Poster of '57 Mustang, leave.

The phone rang while I was sorting through some books. *Treasure Island*, keep. *Bridge to Terabithia*, keep. I heard Mom talking, first slow, then fast. The phone slammed onto the floor, broken pieces scattering on the linoleum. Seconds later she burst into my room. "No time, Megs," she said. "Leave it all. We gotta go *now!*"

I grabbed my backpack and we ran out the door. Three minutes later we were on the freeway headed east out of town. Once we passed the CHICAGO 220 MILES sign, Mom finally relaxed. "Don't worry, Megs," she said, lighting a cigarette and leaning the driver's seat back a little. "It's all going to be okay."

And that's what I'm thinking as I stuff my backpack full of the treasures I found in this SUV. *It's going to be okay.* Spaceballs are shooting death rays from the sky. All I have left to eat is five pieces of popcorn and one tube of ketchup. I'll drink the last of the beer before we leave. Plus I have one hungry kitten—how did I wind up with that? Richie is coming back any minute and he's expecting to find a gun in the safe. A gun that I don't want him to have. Instead he'll find a note from yours truly. But still I whisper, as I roll up my sleeping bag and tie it to my backpack, that it's going to be okay.

I slip the backpack on and step out the door, headed for who knows where. Definitely up because down isn't a choice. I look over my shoulder at Mom's car, all covered with dust, dents, and duct tape. The taillights are broken, pieces of red plastic mixing in with the dirt and cement. I walk into the shadows of the parking garage, a yellow kitten in one hand and a briefcase in the other.

Mom is right. Crazy does run in the family.

- LIGHTS OUT -

"I wouldn't do that," he says. "You're leaving too many pieces open."

"You wouldn't do that," I say, "because you're not a risk taker. Me, on the other hand, I'm fearless."

Of course he rolls double threes, lands on two of my unprotected chips, and knocks them off the board. It's a crushing blow.

He says, "This game is a delicate balance of patience and calculated risks."

I pick up the dice and say, "It's a game of dumb luck, plain and simple."

We're sitting on the family room floor, playing one of my least favorite games of all time—backgammon. Dad's on this board-game kick. Monopoly and Scrabble yesterday, both of which I dominated. Now we're supposedly on his turf. He even played backgammon online, back in the PP (Pre-POD) days. This must be our thousandth game. I had a string of victories this morning, but he's on one of his patented streaks of lucky rolls.

I shake the dice, saying, "If you want a game with real strategy and risks, Halo is the obvious choice."

"Halo?"

"It's what Alex and I play whenever he comes over."

"Ah, the video game."

"It's more than a video game," I say, releasing the dice. "It's a defining—"

The lights go out. No flicker, just out.

The power has been iffy the past couple of days, but it always comes back—sometimes in a couple of seconds, sometimes a couple of minutes. This time is different. I have an odd feeling in my stomach like this is a whole new deal.

We sit in the dark. There's a wind outside. The house creaks.

Somewhere to my right there's a thump—my brain races to catalog the sound. Up high, maybe aliens on the roof, maybe not. Odds are it's a tree branch rubbing up against the house.

I have an unbearable need to hear something other than my screaming mind. "Look," I say, not even able to see the board, "I rolled double sixes!"

"Shhhh!" Dad stands up. The floor creaks as his footsteps move to the patio door. "The whole town is dark," he says.

I'm staring out the window. I've never seen the world so absent of light. No stars, no moon. For all we know, the PODs landed and bug-eyed storm troopers are slithering their way through our neighborhood. I wish Dutch were a Rottweiler, not a house hound with an arthritic hip. When the aliens come he'll wag his tail and lick their tentacles.

Five minutes of this waiting-for-the-world-to-end and my brain is shooting sparks.

"Can I light some candles at least?"

"Might as well," Dad says.

Candles are already strategically placed, so it's just a matter of walking around the room with a lighter. Luckily, Mom was a big fan of candles. The house was beginning to smell pretty stale. The fruity scents provide a welcome relief. In some distant way they remind me of another life.

Dad returns to the floor, scans the board. "It's your move," he says.

He still wants to play the stupid game. "You're not serious," I say.

"You rolled a two-three."

"You're crazy."

"No. I'm winning. You want to roll again?"

I glare at him, afraid of what I'd say if I open my mouth.

He takes one of his deep, thoughtful breaths.

Please, *no! Not the Sphere of Influence speech.*

"Look, we need to keep things as normal as possible, so—"

"Normal?" I say. "*Normal?*" He starts to say something, but I cut him off, the dam really open now. "There's a giant spaceship hovering over my best friend's house. We're like animals in cages and we're all starving! And now we don't have electricity. I'd say *normal* is out the freaking window!"

"It's the way things are, Josh," he says, his voice all calm like he's the therapist and I'm the psycho. "Worrying about it won't accomplish anything."

Worrying? This from the man who invented the concept.

I kick the backgammon board. It slams into the wall, breaking in half and scattering pieces, brown and white, all over the carpet. This feels good for exactly one second.

He starts picking up the pieces. His shadow, stretched out and cartoonish in the candlelight, flickers against the wall.

My voice shaking, I say, "How about if I walk out the door? Go for a little stroll. Maybe visit our friendly neighbors, the Conrads? See how normal things really are."

On his hands and knees and looking at the floor, he says, "You do that, Josh, and I'm right behind you."

Later, I'm trying to find a way to fall asleep. Dad's downstairs playing the piano. He knows only one song, "Blowing in the Wind." Everything else he plays is just notes that occasionally sound like something familiar. He once played this song over and over for two hours after he and Mom had an epic fight. Dad keeps talking about piano lessons, but news flash—he waited too long.

I'm reading People magazine with a flashlight. The issue is only two weeks old. Mel Gibson is on the cover—he has a new war movie that should've opened this month. Britney Spears is pregnant again, or maybe she's just getting fat. I turn the pages but can't focus. The guilt feels like a boil on my brain. I shouldn't have kicked the backgammon board. And then I threatened to walk out the door. Jesus! It was all stupid, every little bit. And Dad would die, me wasting batteries on a magazine like this.

I turn off the flashlight and pull up the covers in the dark with the wind picking up outside, and think about Lynn. I wish I'd kissed her that night after the jazz-band concert. She was sending me every kind of signal—squeezing my hand, pressing her leg against mine, looking at me sideways with her lips parted just a little. I wish I had told her I like the way her hair smells, or put her hand over my heart so she could feel the way it thumps in my chest when she's close. But I waited too long, so there's that, too. I close my eyes, trying to remember her lips and that killer sideways smile, hoping that's the last thing I see before I fall asleep.

But it isn't. Lynn morphs into the apartment girl with the dark eyes that I can't quite see. Instead of sweats she's wearing this amazing white gauzy dress that's almost transparent in the sun. She blows me a long, slow kiss and I feel the warm wetness brushing my skin. This is what my brain grabs onto when I finally drift off to nothing.

- FALLING -

I'm at the top of my world—Level 7. There is a Level 8, but that's on the roof. I'm sure all the cars up there got hit by the death ray, so it may as well be on the moon. That means seven levels of broken glass, crumpled fenders, leaking fluids, and bad smells. I found another bloater on Level 5, a man with a neatly trimmed beard and short gray hair. He was wearing jeans and a pajama top. His legs were pinned between two cars. He wrote *I love you Mary* in the dirt on the trunk of the car in front of him. His eyes were open, just like the grandma bloater's. But this time I climbed onto the hood, held my breath, reached out, and closed his eyes. The lids were cold and stiff and didn't move at first. I found an unopened box of Tic Tacs in his pants pocket. Wintergreen.

I put down the briefcase. My backpack is a little heavier than when I left because I found some treasures on Level 2. I'd like to take it off and rest my shoulders, which are aching big-time, but I may have to leave in a hurry, so I keep it on. Cassie is asleep. I cradle her in my arms while I check out the view. My world has no real walls or windows, just chest-high cement barriers. It's a long way down with nothing to land on but hard pavement and dirt. Maybe some small bushes if I'm lucky. I'd crack like an egg if I jumped.

The sun is beginning to rise in a blue and orange sky with thin clouds crawling left to right. I heard dogs barking earlier this morning, but they're long gone. The only sound I hear is two seagulls screeching from the top of a building nearby. The streets and sidewalks are empty. I close my eyes and imagine the roar of buses and cars and taxi horns and people crowding the sidewalks carrying their Starbucks coffees, walking in and out of stores and talking on cell phones. I open my eyes and—nothing. There must be a wind down there, but I don't feel it. Pieces of paper trash are swirling in a shadowy corner. It's like they're in a dance that spirals them up and up until they either fall or blow away. Where I am the air is cool and still and smells like gasoline.

And of course there's the spaceballs.

Other than disappearing us with their death rays, they don't do anything. What are they waiting for? What happened to the Air Force? The Army? Where's our secret weapon? It's like we've given up. I used to like the movie *Independence Day*. Will Smith is awesome and hot. Now I hate them both.

I count four. Two are huge and round, one is partially hidden by a tall building, one is way off in the distance, a pea-sized dot. They look grayish in the light, not black like I figured. The sun is glinting off the closest one, making it look like giant chrome marble. I think it's spinning but I'm not sure. The weird thing is they're not freaking me out today. They hardly ever flash anymore. Maybe I'm getting used to them. Maybe I'm too hungry and tired to care.

I have to find a place to hide. Levels 3 and 5 have bloaters, so forget them. This level has a few cars—and even a carpet-cleaning van that would have plenty of room—but there just aren't enough choices. Richie would find me for sure. And besides, if I hide up here and need to run, the only direction is down. That makes me too easy to catch. I make up my mind. Level 6 will be my new home. I pop a Tic Tac in my mouth, reach down for the briefcase—

Someone coughs. I freeze.

It's long and loud and coming this way. Hacker! And wherever there's a Hacker, you know there's a Richie. Then I hear him, his gravelly voice sending a chill down my neck: "Cover your damn mouth when you do that! Jesus, get some manners in front of the lady!" Then, "You spit that my way and I'll kill you."

I grab the briefcase and sprint for the nearest car. No time to climb inside. I have to hide underneath. But I stop—the angle is wrong. They could see me on the ground when they come up the ramp. The van would be better, but it's too far. I don't have a choice. Cassie is awake and mewing like crazy. I push the briefcase under the car, then get down on my stomach and crawl like a lizard

71

for the shadows. But my backpack gets hung up on something. I have to let go of Cassie to take off the shoulder straps.

"You *stay!*" I hiss.

They're almost here. Richie laughs at something Hacker says. I wriggle the straps off my shoulders, roll over, and back-crawl into the shadows under the car. I reach out and pull in the pack just as Richie comes around the corner. He's followed by Hacker and someone I'll never forget—the woman with the two kids I saw on the first day. She was driving the SUV when it got smashed. Cassie lets out a string of mews. I roll onto my stomach and stuff her under my arm. She struggles at first, then settles down.

Richie says, "I'd like to believe you, but I don't."

The woman says, "My husband keeps it in a—"

Richie says, "Yeah, you said that already. In a safe under the driver's seat."

The woman says, "Then why are we up here?"

Richie says, "I like the view."

They stop right in front of me, so close I see the scales under the dust on Richie's snakeskin cowboy boots. Hacker has black Nikes with holes in the toes. There's a short gap at his ankles showing a tattoo spiraling up into his pant leg. I think it's a dragon. The woman is wearing sandals—her nails are bright red with chips, like she used to keep them nice but not anymore. Mom was always painting her toenails some crazy color. Black was her favorite. Cassie stirs against my chest. I grip the briefcase and hold my breath.

Richie says, "See, the problem is I broke into that safe this morning, and guess what? No gun."

The woman says, "But he always keeps it there."

Richie says, "All I found is this."

The woman says, "A cell phone? Something's wrong because he keeps cash in there, too."

Hacker says, "Cash? How much?"

The woman says, "A thousand dollars."

Hacker says, "A grand? You holdin' out on me, Richie?"

Richie says, "What the hell's wrong with you I gotta keep repeating myself? I go back to the Navigator, waste two hours of my morning with a hammer and chisel busting out the lock. All I get for my effort is this." He drops the phone, stomps on it with the heel of his boot, grinds it into the cement. "No key. No cash. And no gun."

Hacker says, "Why would he keep just a cell phone in the safe? That don't make sense."

A pause. The boots take a step toward Hacker, then, "What don't make sense is you questioning my integrity. 'Cause if you are, my friend, then we got us a whole new con-versation."

I hear a click. The woman takes a sharp breath, like she was just touched by something cold.

Richie says, "Don't mind me, ma'am. This calms my nerves. It's a technique I learned in anger-management class. Part of my *re*-habilitation."

No one talks.

Then Richie says, "My grandfather gave this to me when I turned sixteen. Must've gutted five hundred elk. Gen-u-ine bleached bone handle from the hip of a twelve-point buck. Carved it himself. I call this move...the slice 'n dice."

Hacker says, "You ever cut your finger doin' those tricks?"

Richie says, "I cut some fingers. Just not my own."

The click again.

Richie says, "There, I feel better now. So where were we? Oh yeah, on the subject of lying. If it's not me and it's not him, then who?"

The woman says, "I...I told you. It's not my fault the gun isn't there." Her voice cracks for the first time. She's trying not to cry, and it's not working. I know what the problem is. She sees what I can't—Richie's eyes, deep in the shadows of that hood.

Hacker says, "Try explaining that to Mr. Hendricks."

Should I come out? Should I tell them who's really lying? Throw the briefcase at Richie and run? No, not yet...

Richie says, "So that's the best you can do?"

The woman says, "Did you find a kitten in a cage? It would be in the back, under a towel."

Richie says, "A safe with no gun. A cage with no kitten. Seems like a trend with you."

The woman says, "Can I please go back to my kids?"

Richie says, "Of course you can. But first we gotta figure this out. Get a new per-spective."

He walks a short distance and stops. He's behind me—I can't see those boots.

Richie says, "You should check out the view from up here."

The woman takes a deep breath, then says, "I'd rather not. I'm afraid of heights."

I grip the handle of the briefcase so hard my knuckles turn white.

Richie says, "There's a little coffee shop used to sell the best huckleberry scones, right up there on Wilshire. Fresh out of the oven, twice a day. It was easy to know when they were comin' out 'cause you'd see a line down the block. Real huckleberries picked in the Willamette Valley in Oregon. I miss little treasures like that."

The sandals don't move.

"C'mon," he says, smooth and easy. "Let's look out over the city, you 'n me. Watch the beautiful alien spaceships, do some brain-storming. We'll figure out a so-lution to this mutual problem."

She's still not moving.

Richie sighs and says, "I'm asking *nice*."

The woman walks toward Richie. I'm facing the wrong direc-tion. I'd make too much noise turning around, so all I do is listen to her sandals drag across the pavement. It's like her feet are too heavy to lift. The sound stops. My legs are numb from lying on the cold cement, and my stomach hurts from trying not to crush Cassie.

The woman says, "I...I don't like this."

Richie says, "Aw, it ain't that bad. Now look right down there, two blocks east—Jake's Java Joint, with the big green sign."

The woman says, "I can't see—"

Richie says, "You gotta lean out a little, like this." A pause. "Yeah, you see it now?"

There's a soft grunt.

The woman says, "*No!* Don't—"

Then a scream, a flash of light. Three heartbeats and it's done. I close my eyes, not wanting to see what I think I heard. There's five seconds of silence. A wave of anger sweeps through me. I could have stopped him! I could have saved her and I didn't. If I knew how to open this briefcase right now, I'd take the gun, point at the center of that hood...

Richie whistles. "You see that, my friend? Didn't even hit the ground. I'm tellin' you, they never miss. Not once!"

Hacker says, "Why'd you do that?"

Richie, the boots walking back to Hacker, says, "It's simple. You lie, you die. That's my motto."

Hacker laughs, which turns into a coughing spasm. It's a bad one.

When he's done, Richie says, "There is one small detail I forgot to mention. This was in the safe."

After a moment, Hacker says, "Bang, bang? Who wrote it?"

"Whoever got to the safe before me."

"So the lady wasn't lying."

"She said there would be a gun and there wasn't. That's close enough." A pause, then, "Why you givin' me that look?"

"Seems like a sad waste, is all."

"Hey, someone's gotta feed the aliens. Otherwise they'll come lookin' for food. Way I see it, I just did humanity a favor."

Hacker spits and says, "You show this note to Mr. Hendricks?"

"Yes."

"What'd he say?"

"Get the gun."

"That's it?"

"More or less. He doesn't want the guests to have it. That point he made very clear."

"You think it's in the hotel?"

"No. Remember I said someone had a nest in the Navigator? Well, all that stuff, the sleeping bag and clothes, a yellow backpack—it's all gone now."

"What're you thinkin'?"

"There's a pirate co-habitating this garage."

"A pirate with a gun."

"According to the note."

"You bring the .45?"

"Wouldn't leave home without it."

"So now what?"

Richie says, "We go on a little treasure hunt. Look for a sleeping bag and a kitten."

They start walking away.

As their voices fade, Hacker says, "The lady said there was a grand in the safe. You happen to see any of that?"

Richie says, "The pirate must've took it."

I wait until I'm sure they're on Level 6. I crawl out from under the car, leaving my backpack and the briefcase where they are. I put Cassie in the back seat—this would be a good time for her to sleep. I don't need to be worrying about a hungry kitten right now. Richie with a knife is bad enough. Now he has a gun. I walk over to the wall, reach into my pocket, and fish out the key to the safe. My mind pictures the woman, her sandals, her painted toes, her two kids back in the hotel. Why did I leave that note? What was I thinking? I throw the key as far as I can. It disappears in the empty streets below. I wait a few seconds, then walk back to the truck.

A plan, which I hope won't be as stupid as it was to leave the note, is forming in my head.

I sneak down the ramp, hugging the wall and staying in shadows as much as I can. Ten more feet and I'm peering around a cement pillar, watching Richie and Hacker look for treasure. Richie stands guard with the .45 while Hacker uses a huge metal rod to pry open the trunks of cars. When they finish with a car they leave the trunk lid open, then move on to the next. There's one car near the far wall, a blue Volvo four-door, with a trunk lid that won't stay up. After a couple of tries Richie says, "Screw it," and they move on to the next victim. This goes on until they've hit every car on this level, twenty at least, pulling all the stuff out, keeping some of it and throwing the rest over the side, with Richie saying, "No point in leaving anything useful for our friend." Finally they move down to the next level. I sneak back to fetch my pack and the briefcase. And Cassie, who misses me, of course.

"Let's check out our new home," I say as she licks my thumb. "It's my favorite color. Blue."

DAY 11: PROSSER, WASHINGTON

- BAM -

"The water is off."

I search for the clock beside my bed. It's off, too—oh, yeah, no power. That would explain why Dad is peering down at me, his head lit up by the candle in his hand. I drag a pillow over my face. He pulls it away.

"No more showers, no more toilet," he says. "We urinate in the green bucket in the garage and defecate in the brown bucket, then toss the contents out the side door in the garage."

I stare at him. He actually said "defecate."

Sitting up I say, "So our yard is the toilet?"

"We don't have a choice."

"You woke me up to tell me this?"

"I needed to catch you before you went to the bathroom."

Whatever time it is, it's way too early for words like "defecate," or to think about color-coded buckets of crap and how our life has just slipped down another notch. I roll over, facing the wall. "I'm going back to sleep," I say.

He's still there. I feel him in the room. After a few moments he says, "There's something else I need to say."

"Can't it wait until the sun comes up?" I ask.

"No."

"Okay, so say it already."

"You know that rule I made about Mom?" he asks.

"The one where we're not supposed to talk about her?"

"It's a stupid rule," he says.

"You can say that again," I say, looking at the wall.

Mercifully, the door clicks and he's gone.

The clock on top of the piano runs on a battery, so it's one of two ties we have to life PP (Pre- POD). My Seiko is in my locker at school. Dad has a Timex digital that he wears constantly, but he's spending more and more time in his room. My old standbys, the displays on the microwave and cable TV box, are useless. But that doesn't stop me from checking them at least fifty times a day. If time flies when you're having fun, it moves like a tree sloth when you're not.

So the piano clock says 2:30 in the afternoon. I've been trying to find the apartment girl pretty much nonstop since breakfast. Nothing but the usual suspects scratching their butts. I pick up the binoculars, sit down in the chair, put my feet up, and scan to the third floor.

Showtime! She's standing at the window.

She holds a sheet of paper against the glass. In thick black letters it reads:

HT IM Amanda

It's text-message for *Hi there, I'm Amanda*. I motion for her to wait, then tear through the house, snagging a stack of paper from the useless printer in Dad's office and a marking pen from the utility drawer. But the top's off the pen, so the ink is dried out. I run around opening and slamming drawers, waking Dutch and getting the raised hairy eyebrow from Dad. I find a bazillion markers, but they're all too thin. She'd never see them. Finally I track down a thick marker in the closet with all the present-wrapping supplies. This one works, so I run back to the window. She's waiting, but she seems anxious, looking over her shoulder. I write in big letters, asking her, *How's it going?*

Me: IM josh HIG?

She puts down her binoculars and replies.

Amanda: IM starving.

Is she really starving, or just saying it? It's hard to tell with those sweats she's wearing. I'm not skin-and-bones starving, but the refrigerator is empty and we're eating from cans. I write, *Me too. Let's order some pizza.*

Me: M2 lets order za

Amanda: ROFL RU scared?

Rolling on floor laughing. Are you scared? Yeah, well, only all the time, except when I'm doing this. Or sleeping. I wonder if she knows there's a POD right over her apartment. Then I wonder if there's a POD over our house. I answer, *Scared of what? Just kidding.*

Me: scared of what? JK

Amanda: RU alone?

Me: no. stuck w/dad n dog RU?

Amanda: no IWIWU

I wish I was you. That's what *she* thinks—she doesn't know my dad. But I wonder about the skinny dude.

Me: Y?

Amanda: he stole r food n watr n beer :(

Me: he?

Amanda: BAM w/gun

I'm pretty sure I know what this means. Since he stole her stuff and has a gun, I'm guessing *badass man.* I get a memory flash of the man on the sidewalk—small round holes leaking streaks of red. This skinny dude needs to go. The marker shakes in my hand as I write.

Me: where is he now?

Amanda: ZZZZ

Sleeping. I wonder where her parents are.

Me: where r yr rents?

Amanda: KIA

Killed in action? By the PODs or the skinny guy? I keep it simple for now.

Me: :(

Amanda: my lil sis is sik.

My little sister is sick. This keeps getting worse. I think about it, then write, *Sucks to be you. Call for help.*

Me: S2BU 911!

Amanda: LOLA URYY4M

Laughing out loud again. I need to think on the second part. *You are...something...for me.* But what's up with the two Y's? Then I get it. Too wise! *You are too wise for me.* I look at her. She's holding up another sheet of paper, glancing over her shoulder. It looks like the monster is waking.

Amanda: GTGB

Got to go, bye. She scoops up her papers, blows me a kiss, and is gone.

She blew me a kiss! Just like in my dream. My head spins. I want to run over there and kick the skinny guy's ass. But I can't do that either. So I sit in my comfy chair, feet up on the ottoman, and quietly resist the urge to throw the binoculars through the window.

I must have fallen asleep—it's dark outside. The clock reads 7:23. I stand up, stretch, and walk into the kitchen. Dad is sitting at the dining room table, punching numbers into a calculator by candlelight. His POD notebook is open; he's working on yet another graph, no doubt. I know he's had dinner—there's a spicy smell that's vaguely familiar. The counters are spotless. I wonder if he used some of our precious water to clean them.

Dad takes off his glasses and says, "Well, someone's had a busy day." He smiles, hoping for more.

I shrug. "All this activity wears me out."

Still hopeful, he says, "You empty every drawer in the house and that's all I get?"

I pick up his pen, flip to an empty page in his notebook, and write: NIYWFD. *Never in your wildest freaking dreams.* "Figure that out and I'll tell all."

He puts his glasses on, studies the page. I sit at the table and watch. His lips are moving, sounding things out. The gears are really spinning. He writes down a couple of words, not even close. After a minute he says, "Do I get a clue?"

"Ha! In your dreams!"

It's his turn to shrug. He says, "You hungry?"

"I could eat."

"Well, tonight's menu features a can of chili or a can of clam chowder. I recommend the chili. The chowder is supposed to use milk."

That's an easy one. I hate clams. "I guess it's chili," I say.

"Would you like it hot? I'll fire up the camp stove if—"

"No thanks. I prefer my chili cold and congealed."

"Okay then." He gets up, starts for the pantry.

"Hold on. I'll manage this one," I say. "You sit down, work on that puzzle."

He returns to the table. I snag a can of chili from the pantry, open it, dump the contents into a bowl. It sits there in a lumpy brown and red pile. Now I recognize the mystery smell. Chili seasonings and beans sear my nostrils. Dutch, unaffected, is up and drooling on my foot.

Dad, back to the riddle, says, "Not In Your Wacky Friend's Dorm?"

I hear him but I don't. I'm staring at the bowl, thinking: *I can't believe I told her to call 911. I'm an idiot!* I poke at the glop with a spoon. It makes a sucking sound that reminds me of a bodily function. Whatever appetite I had is out the window.

Suddenly the brown bucket is calling.

Dad says, "You look a little green in the gills. Would you like a baggie of water?"

"I'll eat this later," I say, knowing that will never happen. "Right now I need to make my donation to the neighborhood beautification project."

Considering the events of the day, this seems like the right thing to do.

- MY NEW ADDRESS -

This is my new address:

Megs Moran
Level 6 Orange
Row J, Space 12
Los Angeles, California

Here are the directions. You go to Level 6 Orange—orange be-cause all the levels have different colors. If you have kids, avoid the bloaters on Levels 3 and 5. The smell is so bad they might puke. Find Row J—you can't miss it, there's a little brown Toyota truck at the front with muddy monster tires that Richie slashed. Walk all the way down to space 12, that's two cars up from the end. If you go too far you'll be staring at three huge spaceballs. I'm next to the white Ford Focus with dangling side mirrors (be careful not to step on the broken glass—there's lots of it). Knock three times on the trunk of the blue Volvo. I'll pop out like a weasel and say, *Nice to see you!*—unless you're Richie or Hacker, in which case I'll scream my head off. Like I did an hour ago when I woke up from a dream about Richie cutting into the trunk with a chainsaw.

I like my new home. It smells nice, like leather and perfume. A thin beam of early-morning sun is shining in through a broken window. The front seat is my dining room—that's where I would eat if I had any food. The back seat is my living room—that's where I stretch out and read the *Alien vs. Predator* comic book for the fiftieth time or play with Cassie when she has the energy. The trunk is my bedroom—that's where I sleep. It's really dark in there. My bedroom has two exits, one through the back seat, which folds down, and the other through the trunk lid, which Hacker busted with his metal rod. I hang out in the back seat—

excuse me, living room—and scurry like a squirrel into the trunk whenever I hear a noise. Which is almost all the time. I tied a piece of string to the inside of the back seat so I can close it from inside the trunk. I've got it down to five seconds. Richie won't even know I'm here.

After the dream I couldn't get back to sleep. That's two nights in a row of not sleeping, and it's wearing me down. I'm so thirsty I can't lick my lips. I finished the water just a minute ago, two sips for me, one for Cassie. It didn't help. My stomach is cramping and I'm starting to smell like a bloater. I look in the rearview mirror. A wild animal stares back at me. Dirty face streaked with engine oil, red zombie eyes, hair like a bird's nest. If Mom saw me now she'd run away or probably just die. It's official. I'm a total cave troll.

To cheer myself up I open my backpack and empty the treasures I've found onto the seat. Mom was a big fan of writing things down, so I make a list.

Stuff I Have
2 screwdrivers, 1 Phillips, 1 flat.
1 sleeping bag
1 pair smashed glasses
1 cigarette lighter
1 flashlight pen
1 pocketknife with a broken blade
2 nearly empty packs of cigarettes
1 sm. bottle with 18 pills (azithro-something)
1 makeup mirror, 2 tubes red lipstick, a hairbrush
3 comic books (2 Spiderman, 1 Alien vs. Predator),
2 totally empty water bottles
2 paper clips, 1 sewing needle, 1 thing of yellow thread
2 bites of chocolate (thanks to Grandma Bloater!)
1 kitten
1 briefcase
1 gun (I think)

Then I make another list.

Stuff I Need
Food and water
Toilet paper
Toothbrush and toothpaste
A shower
Shampoo with conditioner
More chocolate
I really, really like chocolate.

So now what? I try opening the briefcase but can't pop the lock with a screwdriver. I decide it's not safe to keep the case in the car, so I hide it under the trash in the garbage can next to the green door. I could try sneaking into the hotel, but I don't like that idea—too many scary people come out of those green doors. I'd rather take my chances in here. But I have to do something. The food I have left wouldn't fill a Dixie cup. I heard the body can live without food for days, maybe even weeks, but I don't know about water. It *seems* like less—a lot less. I think Cassie is starving, too. There's nothing but bone under skin when I pet her. She hardly ever wants to play anymore. I know I should get supplies, but my heart isn't in it. I have this creepy feeling that Richie set a trap. He's waiting around the next corner, behind the next car. And when he catches me he's going to take the metal case. And then he's going to feed me to the aliens. Every time I close my eyes I see his snakeskin boots. I hear that lady scream "No!" just before the flash of light. So I don't do anything.

It's like I'm a long-necked chicken. I sit in my new home waiting for the farmer with the ax.

- BLUE-LIGHT SPECIAL -

The screeching sound again, this time in the middle of the night. I twist like a worm on a hook in my bed, then pull my knees up to my chest and wait for it to end. Or wait to die—whichever comes first.

It stops, sort of.

A blue light seeps into my room. At first it's just a curiosity, maybe a reflection off something. But within seconds I know it's something much bigger. It fills my room. The light is so intense that my eyelids can't stop it. And my hands—I see the veins, like I'm turning into some translucent jellyfish. This can be only one thing. I get out of bed and look out the window. The PODs are glowing, each one as bright as a blue sun. It hurts to look at them, even for a second.

Dad slams into my room. He isn't wearing a shirt. I see through his skin to shadowy organs underneath. Liver, kidney, a pulsing heart. His head is a screaming skull.

"Don't look at them, Josh! Don't look!"

The light turns off. It lasted what, fifteen, twenty seconds? Add the ten seconds of screeching brain torture and the whole experience lasted maybe half a minute. That's thirty seconds of the aliens yanking our chain. Of the POD commander having a little fun, shaking our cages, making sure the humans don't get too comfortable or feel too safe. Now my room is completely black, except for the lingering blue globs I see when I close my eyes.

Dad, his brain no longer visible, says, "Where's your flashlight?"

"On my nightstand."

I grope around, find it, thumb the switch. It doesn't work.

"Huh," I say. "It was working fine when I went to bed."

He says, "I'll get the one in the hall closet."

He walks away, his hand sliding along the wall. I look out the window again. The PODs are back to normal—meaning I barely see them. They're black holes in a moonless, star-filled sky. In the far-off distance a coyote yaps, then more chime in. I guess they didn't like the show either. Or maybe they did.

Dad walks into the room carrying a lit candle.

"Couldn't find the flashlight?" I say.

"It didn't work."

He stands beside me at the window. I get a sudden flash of déjà vu. The two of us in my room, trying to figure out what the hell happened. It makes me shiver.

He says, "Looks like our guests have gone back to sleep." That's his latest word for them—guests. And we're the hosts. Like this is Uncle Charlie, Auntie El, and their obnoxious twins visiting from East Lansing. I told him it's more like Masters and Bitches, and guess who we are? He said, "To quote one of your generation's favorite phrases, 'whatever.'"

"They never sleep," I say.

He nods.

"What time is it?" I ask.

He looks at his watch. "That's strange."

"What is?"

"The display—it's dead." He shakes his wrist, checks the watch again, presses some buttons, frowns.

I say, "I'll get my cell." It shows the time on the cover. At least it did the last time I checked. I've got a sinking feeling that things are different now. I pull it out of my dresser drawer. Feeling confirmed. "Nada," I say.

He hands me the candle, goes to my desk, and picks up the chair. He carries it to the middle of the room, stands on it, reaches up, and pushes the test button on the smoke alarm. It's wired into the household circuit, but also has a battery backup. He changes all the batteries four times a year, like clockwork, so it should be fresh. We should hear an angry three-second blast, a pleasant bird-song compared to the alien screech. Nothing happens.

"Maybe it was some kind of electromagnetic pulse," he says. *And maybe they're getting ready to kick our ass.* I say, "It was crazy, Dad. I could see your heart beating."

"And you didn't have any eyeballs."

That's a vision I'd rather not think about.

We stand there for a few seconds, neither of us saying anything. Then he says, "Looks like the show's over," and turns to leave.

"Now what?"

"I'm going downstairs to check on a few things."

"Make an entry in your notebook, perhaps?"

He smiles. "Yeah, that too."

This is crazy. A week ago he'd be at Defcon 5, running around trying to board up the windows. Now he's all calm, as if a blue light that turns us into talking skeletons is nothing special. Something doesn't add up.

"I think I'll hang here for a while," I say, not that into making sure there are still three cans of mushroom soup in the pantry. "Let me know if there's a problem with Dutch."

He stops at the door and says, "You know, Josh, with the smoke detectors not working, it might be better if you—"

"I know, I know. Don't use the candle in my room because I might fall asleep and burn the house down."

"I'll follow the same rule," he says.

"Safety first!" I call to his retreating steps.

He walks downstairs. I blow out the candle. I crawl into bed, pull up the covers, and ponder this new reality. Even when the power was out, we still had batteries. The house had a pulse. Now it just feels dead. The simple truth hits me like a brick: I have over fifteen thousand songs on my iPod, and I may never hear a single one of them again.

Dad breaks the news to me over breakfast. The electromagnetic pulse, or whatever it was, is probably permanent. Nothing works, not even the tiny light on Mom's keychain.

We're sharing a can of mini-sausages when he says, out of the blue, "You know what else uses a battery?"

I think for a moment, scratch my head. "No!" I say with a fake gasp. "Not the TV remote?"

He smiles, but it's the kind that takes some effort. Like when someone goes, *Say cheese!* and you smile, but all you want to do is poke them in the eye with a cue stick. A couple of other wise-ass comments come to mind, but I don't say them. I fork the last sausage, dip it in the almost-empty jar of deli mustard, pop it into my mouth, and wait. I know it's coming—it's gonna be good. Something real useful, like the battery to his GPS. Or his shaver. The suspense is killing me...

"My pacemaker," he says, looking me straight in the eyes.

DAY 13: LOS ANGELES, CALIFORNIA

- BLINDED BY THE LIGHT -

I'm in the trunk. The back seat is open a crack so I can get some air. I can't keep the seat totally closed because then it feels like I'm sleeping in a coffin. I'm doing something that I shouldn't be doing—reading a comic book with my flashlight pen. I shouldn't be wasting the batteries over something as stupid as *Alien vs. Predator*, but when my stomach is growling so loud I can't sleep, it really helps to think about something else. Even if it's killer space creatures with acid for blood and spider-faced warriors that hunt humans and hang their chopped-off heads like trophies from trees. I whisper a promise to the furball sleeping at my feet—"One more page, just one more...then I'll turn off the light."

I don't get the chance.

The screaming demons come back. It's the same awful sound that exploded in my head just before the spaceballs attacked. I look at Cassie—she's still sleeping. How is this possible? I can hardly breathe. I need more air. But if I open the seat maybe the sound will be even louder? I decide it doesn't matter if I'm dead. I clamp the flashlight pen between my teeth, punch down the seat, and crawl outside. It makes no difference because the demons aren't outside. They're screaming in my head.

And then they stop.

The garage is dark, except for the thin beam coming from my flashlight. I blink, take some deep breaths. A soft blue light is coming inside from beyond the wall. It gets brighter and brighter. Then everything is blue. I know it's the spaceballs. I reach out for the door handle and choke back a scream. My hands—I can almost see through them all the way to the bones. It's like I'm disappearing! And my eyes feel like they're on fire. I dive back into the trunk and lift up the seat. But my sleeping bag is wedged in the opening. It won't close. I kick the seat down, which lets in more light. Cassie hisses at me.

She looks normal. Why isn't she disappearing?

And then the light goes off.

But not just the blue light—all light, everywhere. Even my pathetic little flashlight pen. It makes no difference if my eyes are open or closed. Am I blind?

All I can think of is, the aliens are coming. They used the demons to wake us up, then the blue light to blind us. Now they're attacking. I try to think of places to hide, but what's the point? I can't go anywhere because I can't see. I might as well stay where I am. I reach out for Cassie, find her. She mews softly as I pull her close. I duck my head into the sleeping bag—the two of us alone in the swallowing dark. Waiting for monsters to find us. For tentacles to slide in through the windows and wrap around the sleeping bag and lift me screaming out of the car. I wish it was a dream, but I know it's not.

The gun! If only I could use the gun!

Then I think, Like that's going to help. A blind girl shooting in the dark at slimy tentacles that could probably crush this car. Brilliant! My ears grab on to every sound. Every tick, click, or rustling whisper of wind. And in the middle of all this, Cassie starts purring. Her tongue, small like a fingernail and sandpaper rough, licks my face. I realize I'm crying. "Stop that noise!" I whisper. "The aliens will hear you."

But Cassie doesn't care about the drooling monsters. She doesn't care about the fangs or the yellow eyes glowing over the trunk. All she cares about is licking the tears streaming down my face. I take a deep breath and use the rhythm of Cassie's motor to settle me down. After a moment or two I have another thought—one that makes me smile.

"Who knows?" I whisper. "Maybe the aliens are allergic to cats."

- WICKED EVIL GRIN -

Amanda: SUP?

What's up? How about "I'm too busy to pee"?

Me: IM2BZ2P

Amanda: LHO URAQT

Laughing head off. You are a cutie. I'm liking the sound of this.

Me: SUP w/U?

Amanda: out of TP

Out of toilet paper? Ha! I can fix that.

Me: use $$$

Amanda: YUK!!!!!

She's in a good mood. Not always looking over her shoulder. She's wearing a purple University of Washington sweatshirt. It's a little on the baggy side, but she makes it work.

Me: UR happy 2day?

Amanda: yes!!! BAM is KIA

The skinny dude is dead? Cool. Right away I wonder, did she do it?

Me: was it U?

Amanda: WEG

Wicked evil grin. She starts another sheet of paper, so I wait.

Amanda: 2 men tak hm awy n

And another...

Amanda: bring us food/watr/meds

Me: gr8 news!

Amanda smiles. Actually "beams" is a better word. She claps her hands and spins. It's like the goblin king just died.

Amanda: thx. RUOK?

Thanks. Are you OK? Not much going on here, except the news about Dad's pacemaker. I decide not to rain on her parade. Besides, how do you text "pacemaker"?

Me: SSDD

Amanda looks puzzled.

Amanda: WDYMBT?

What do you mean by that? She doesn't know SSDD? Dad walks into the room. He stands in front of the window, facing the apartments across the street. Maybe he sees her, but I doubt it. He reaches down his sweatpants and absently scratches his balls. *Jesus!* I look back up at Amanda. She's writing, shaking her head.

Amanda: ewww!!! PIR?

Parent in room? Maybe she means, *Perv in room?* If only she knew. It doesn't look like the ball scratcher is about to leave anytime soon, so I write, "Bye for now."

Me: sorry. B4N.

Amanda: L8R

Later. She waves and walks away. What? No kiss? This sucks.

Dad picks up the sheet of paper on the floor with "SSDD" on it. He asks me what it means.

I say, "Take a wild guess."

"Sad Santa disco-dances?"

I say, "Guess again."

He says, "Same shit, different day."

My mouth drops open. He smiles, hands me the paper, and walks away.

DAY 15: LOS ANGELES, CALIFORNIA

- MY LUCKY DAY -

Good news: I'm not blind.

Bad news: I'm totally out of food and water. Not a drop, not a crumb. I can't sit in this car any longer. I have two hungry mouths to feed. But first I need to think about the dream I had last night. It was so good I don't want to let it go.

Mom and I are on the way to the ocean. She's driving. We're in a red convertible, a BMW I think, with the top down. The sun is shining warm and yellow in a clear blue sky—there aren't any space-balls anywhere. "Little Surfer Girl" is playing on the stereo and we're singing along. In real life I don't know the words, but this is a dream, so I do. Our hair is flying behind us in the breeze, and I'm wearing a pair of corny but very cool heart-shaped sunglasses. Mom points to a bunch of dots in the sky—at first I think they're spaceballs, but it turns out they're really kites with long red tails. Mom says we're close, any second we'll see it—the ocean. In real life I've never jumped in a wave, never even seen the ocean. So I stand on the seat, hands gripping the windshield and face in the wind—this is a dream, so I can do that—and look and look, but it's just out of sight. But I smell it and taste it, the salt, the hot dogs, the suntan oil. Mom yells into the wind that we're going roller-skating and buying fresh-squeezed raspberry lemonades. We're going to smear ourselves with coconut oil and get tanned like movie stars! Then someone in the car in front of us throws a can of soda out the window. Mom yells, "Megs! Watch out!" but I just smile down at her and do nothing, and even though it's going in slow motion, the can hits me in the head.

That's what wakes me up—I bumped my head on the roof of the trunk. I have a little bruise on my forehead, but it reminds me of the dream, so I don't mind. At first I had a headache too, but now it's gone.

The sun is high enough now that I can see what I'm doing, but there's still plenty of good shadows for hiding. I figure it's best if

I don't keep the briefcase with me, so I leave it buried under the trash. I hide my treasures in the trunk in a secret storage place under the carpet, next to the spare tire. Cassie is curled up on top of my sleeping bag. She's peed on it at least twice, but who cares? I'm the only one that smells it. I stuff the empty water bottles in my backpack, slide my shoulders through the straps, and start walking. My destination: Level 1. I'll work my way up from there.

Halfway down I remember that I left the *Alien vs. Predator* comic on the front seat. I don't have the energy to hike all the way back, so I tell myself it's no big deal. Richie won't notice. Everything else is hidden in a trunk he's already searched.

Level 1 is bad news. There's this awful nasty smell, like a backed-up toilet. It doesn't take long to figure out where it's coming from. The green door opens. I duck behind a car and watch a woman and a little girl walk into the garage. The woman is carrying a bucket and a rag. The woman stands in front of the girl while she drops her pants and squats over the bucket. When she's finished she wipes herself with the rag. Then the woman plugs her nose, picks up the bucket, lifts the top to the big green garbage can, and dumps in the contents, rag and all. She knocks on the door. It swings open and they walk inside. So Level 1 has a new name: The Sewer.

I get all choked when I sit in our old car. It's covered with even more dust. The clock that Mom bought at a Wal-Mart in Nebraska on the second day of our trip is on the floor. I look at it and keep seeing the two of us escaping Zack and taking off on our great adventure. That was fun. Scary, but fun. I look around for a note. Nothing but more dust.

I walk to my second home, the SUV. It's a horror show. Someone, or *something*, ripped it to shreds. Hmm...I wonder who that could be. It looks like it was attacked by tigers with chainsaws. All the seats are slashed and the roof liner is pulled down. Too many memories here. Cassie's cage is on the ground, bent and broken. I promise myself not to come back to this spot...ever.

If Level 1 was a bust, then Level 2 is a gold mine. With all the trunks open it's easier for me to search the nooks and crannies, the places Richie and Hacker were too stupid or lazy to look. I find a bag of pistachio nuts stuffed in a tennis shoe, and a short tube of Pringles potato chips under some jumper cables. But the showstopper is a big old Suburban that Richie and his gang have worked over so many times it looks like it's been through a war. The spare, which is slashed—Richie must have a thing about slashing tires—is bolted to the back door, which is unlocked. It's pretty much empty except for jumper cables and a couple of STP oil cans. I'm about to give up when I notice that the carpeting has a seam down the middle and there's a spot in the back corner where it's loose, so I give it a pull. It's held in place with strips of Velcro that keep peeling back and back until I see a black wooden door. I lift up the door. At first I think it's just a bigger-than-normal compartment for the spare tire. But on this car the spare tire is kept outside. I poke my head into the space, and that's when I know I found it—the jackpot.

It's like a small cave. Definitely not as high as the Volvo trunk—when I scrunch down flat the ceiling is two inches from my face. But it's a wide enough for two of me with my legs almost stretched out. There's a thin foam pad on the floor that smells like beer and even small air holes drilled in the top. But the mother lode of them all is wrapped in a smelly horse blanket hidden in the far back. Three packs of Winston cigarettes, five emergency glow sticks, a first-aid kit with six PowerBars, maps of California, Oregon, and Washington, and a small container of pepper spray. I dig a little more and find a roll of ten twenty-dollar bills, two motorcycle magazines (both in Spanish), an opened package of spicy-hot beef jerky, and last but not least: two plastic freezer bags stuffed with marijuana. Or, like Zack called it, weed.

I know weed when I see it. Zack took me with him when he bought it from a guy named Cal behind the PetSmart. He told me that taking a kid along makes the cops less suspicious. And he also told me that if I ever told Mom what we really did on these "trips to the pet store" he'd make me wish I didn't have a mouth. Then he'd smile and buy me an ice cream on the way home. Zack would have done a belly flop onto a bed of nails for the smelly, dried-up leaves in this freezer bag.

I jam some of the loot into my backpack, but not all of it. The PowerBars, pistachio nuts, Pringles, and one glow stick I stash in the hiding place. Oh, and the weed. Like, what am I going to do with that? The wooden door drops into place, the carpet seals, and the cave is closed. I used to dream about that when Zack was drunk, a secret hideout or cave I could use to disappear. *Well, I think with a smile, now I have one.*

But I still don't have what I need most.

Water.

I hike all the way back to Level 6. I'm tempted to just crash and chow down on the beef jerky, but I know it will make me thirstier. From here I can see the Volvo. Everything looks okay, so I keep on marching up to Level 7. I haven't searched any of those cars, plus I remember some kind of cleaning van that might have something useful. So far no sign of Richie. Today is turning out to be my lucky day.

There's a bad memory on Level 7—at the place behind the truck where Richie killed the woman who wore the sandals. I didn't see her face then, but I remember her from the first day. I think about her two kids. Even though I shouldn't, I walk to the wall and look over the edge. It's so far down it makes me dizzy. This is the last thing she saw. If it weren't for me being so stupid, she might still be alive. At least she didn't hit the ground. Maybe that's a good thing. I see the sign for Jake's Java Joint. It's green, just like Richie said.

The cars aren't much help. Richie and Hacker really did a number up here. It's just like all the others—a crumb here, a crust there. All pretty much empty. I find a piece of rock-hard gum chewed up and wadded into a tissue. I try chewing it but can't work up the saliva, so I stuff it in my pocket. The truck I hid under has a silver thermos on the seat. I wonder how Richie missed that one. I shake it. There's something wet inside! When I finally open the top the stink is so bad I almost throw up. I figure they left it there on purpose, hoping I'd be so desperate I'd drink it, puke my guts out, and die.

My last hope is the van. It has *Wave Rider Carpet Cleaning* painted on the side door in big red and black letters that form a circle. Inside the circle is a cartoon of a carpet-cleaning guy on a surfboard saying "Ride the Wave and Save!" The door is hanging open by a crack. I slide it open all the way and climb inside. My heart sinks. There are three carpet-cleaning machines, lots of hoses and cords tossed around, two big orange buckets, and some blue jugs that say either Spotter or Cleaning Solution. I open one of the jugs, take a sniff—it's worse than the thermos. My eyes start watering, which I think is because of the smell, but once my shoulders start shaking and my legs go wobbly, I know what's going on. I'm crying. I sit down between the chords and brushes and orange buckets and let it happen. It's the first time in a long time.

After a while I'm done. Really done.

I'm a total failure. All these cars and I can't find anything to drink. I don't want to go into the hotel, but now it looks like it's my only choice. I stand up, step out of the van, start walking. I'm thinking about Mom and how after a fight with Zack she once told me, "The juice isn't worth the squeeze." I didn't know what she meant then, but I do now. All this work—is it worth it? Just to end up alone, sleeping in trunks that make my hair stink like spare tires and motor oil? Maybe if I go into the hotel I could be sleeping in a real bed. Maybe Mom is in there and Richie isn't letting her out. There's a thought, but I doubt it. And who is this Mr. Hendricks? Why do Richie and Hacker seem so afraid of him?

I kick at a piece of glass, miss—and stop. Thinking of Mom reminded me of something. One time she rented a carpet shampooer. I read the directions to her from the manual while she filled the machine. I remember that it had two containers, or "reservoirs," one for shampoo and one for clean water. Maybe the machines in the van work the same way.

I run back to look. Two of the machines are empty, but the third one has a reservoir with some clear liquid. I yank the hose off the reservoir and smell inside. Not great, not awful. I put a finger in and taste. Water! Warm, wonderful water. I manage to fill two water bottles and half of another.

After guzzling the half bottle, I rip open the package of jerky and wolf down a huge peppery chunk. My mouth burns, but it tastes as good as a T-bone steak. I wash it down with a huge glug of warm, delicious water. I could eat the whole package right now, but I don't. Cassie is waiting back at home and I need to share. I need to make it last. I poke my head out of the van, make sure Richie isn't around, then take off for Level 6. On the way down I keep thinking about Cassie licking water out of my hand.

Something is wrong. I stop and peek around a concrete pillar at the Volvo, which is at the opposite end of the garage. For one thing, the trunk lid is higher than I left it. And the side-view mirror by the driver's door wasn't broken and hanging by a wire. The garbage can by the green door looks the same. No one is around that I see, and I don't hear anyone hacking up a lung, but I don't take any chances. I crouch behind the pillar and watch. And wait.

It's dark now except for a pale silvery light from a rising moon. The air is cold and a wind's coming up. My body is stiff from sitting on the pavement and my teeth are chattering. I need to get back to Cassie and make sure she's okay. I can't wait any longer. It's time to crawl into my warm sleeping bag and eat some dinner. I like the sound of that—dinner. Wherever Richie is, he's not here.

I move low in the shadows, hiding behind every second or third car. There's no sound except my breathing and a loud crunch once when I step on a big piece of glass. It takes a while, but I reach the Volvo. I open the rear door—and scream.

I can't help myself. I bury my head in my sleeve and hope that it muffles the sound that pours from me like liquid pain. The seats are slashed; the stuffing is pulled out and spread around. I dive into the trunk, my hands reaching out like wild things in the dark. The sleeping bag is gone. My notebook is ripped up, the pages in ragged pieces.

And Cassie—Cassie is gone.

There's a note on the dashboard. I can barely read it in the moonlight through my tears:

Dear Parking Garage Pirate—
You have something that belongs to me. Bring
the gun and we'll make a trade. Knock on the door on
level 1 and ask for me. You know who I am. XOXO,
R. PS: Guess what I've got. Meow! Meow!

DAY 16: PROSSER, WASHINGTON

- FILTER FACE -

Again, the screeching. It's beginning to feel like a fire drill—
with one major difference. In the old days, say, like *two weeks ago*,
you'd go outside in a fire drill. Now, it's go outside and you're POD
meat. Of course this fire drill is in the middle of the night, or
maybe early morning—without a watch, who knows? So I have no
clue what's going on. There was a full moon last night, but there
must be heavy-duty clouds because it's like someone tossed a blanket over the house. Occasionally I see a kind of flash, low, like a
camera close to the ground. We'll just have to wait and see what
the POD commander has in store for us today. I can hardly wait.

We know the answer as soon as the sun comes up. Fog. And
not your usual run-of-the-mill, can't-see-the-house-next-door fog.
It's some weird alien thing that's scary as hell. It's so thick we can't
see past the windows. Dad and I stand in front of the patio door,
watching it curl and coil within itself, throbbing with flashes of
internal light, moving like it's alive. For some strange reason Dutch
wants to go outside. Like I'm going to let that happen.

Dad says not to move, he'll be right back. I stare at the freak
show and wonder, What the hell? What could possibly be next? No
water. No power. No cars. And now we can't see out the windows?
Then I think—no more texting with Amanda. I'm ready to punch
my fist through the door when a muffled voice says, "Pood thith
on."

Dad's wearing an air filter, the kind he uses when he's painting
the house or working in the garage turning perfectly good wood
into sawdust. He hands me one of the same.

"Why?" I say.

"Just do it."

"Not until you tell me why."

"Because maybe it's not fog."

"Yeah?"

He sighs through the mask.

"Maybe it's...maybe it's a nerve agent."

My heart kicks into turbo. "You mean a gas? Like they're *gassing* us?"

"It's a possibility."

I grab the filter, slide it over my nose and mouth, stretch the elastic band around my head.

He says, "You feeling any numbness in your fingers or toes?"

"No. You?"

"Not yet. Do you see any blood coming out of my ears?" He shows me one ear, then the other.

"No."

He examines me. "Nothing yet." He takes off his glasses and says, "See any blood dripping from my eyes?"

"No! Jesus, Dad! Are you crazy?"

He says, "One of the first signs of nerve gas is blood leaking out of body orifices."

"Well, if you're trying to scare me, mission freaking accomplished!"

That shuts him up. We stand there looking out at the swirling gray, two housebound humans with cheesy face filters you can buy at Wal-Mart for a buck twenty-five. If this is really nerve gas, then what we really need is a freaking spacesuit. And that makes me think: If these pathetic things actually work, then the PODs screwed this one up big-time.

Dutch presses his nose to the glass. He lets out a long, sad whimper. I haven't seen him like this in a long time. He really wants to go out there. I wonder if Dad has a filter for him.

A small bird lands on the back of a patio chair. It's only two feet from where we're standing, a smudge of brown in a sea of gray. Three blinks later and it flies off.

"I guess it's not *bird agent*," I say.

Dad says, "Maybe it's human-specific. They're obviously leaving animals alone."

I point to Dutch. "So you think we can let him outside in that stuff?"

"Why?"

"You want him to take a whiz on your foot?"

"That would mean opening the door."

"Dad, what have we got to lose?" His eyes narrow above the mask. "I mean, if this is a human-specific nerve agent, we're going to die soon enough anyway. We might as well save Dutch the embarrassment of peeing on the carpet."

"All right," Dad says in a surprise move. "But do it quick and hold your breath."

"Should I get the rope?" These days we don't let Dutch outside unless he's tied to a long rope. That way he won't wander off.

"No," he says. "We wouldn't be able to seal the door."

"Good point."

I wrap my fingers around the handle, undo the latch. Dutch perks his ears, stands up, and wags his tail. He thinks we're going for a walk. Yeah, right. I count to three and open the door just wide enough for a fat old Lab to waddle through.

Two things happen.

The first thing is that Dutch is literally swallowed by the fog. It closes in around him and turns a darker shade of gray. Next there are all these small bursts of electricity that move up and then down his body, like he's being *scanned*.

It's over in ten seconds. Dutch is oblivious. He disappears into the gray.

Dad and I look at each other. Suddenly my eyes roll back into my head. I clutch at my throat and collapse to the floor. I rip off my filter and gasp for air, kicking my legs like I'm in one giant spasmodic convulsion of death.

Dad kneels beside me, his hands pressing down on my shoulders screaming, "Josh! Josh! Take it easy! Relax! Try to breathe! Oh, Jesus!"

There's so much pain—so much pain in his voice that I have to stop. He has a pacemaker with a dead battery. I shouldn't be doing this to him. I sit up and say, "I'm just messin' with you, Dad. I'm fine."

He tears the mask off his face. I swear the look he gives me could melt lead. For a second I think he's going to actually haul off and hit me. Then, out of nowhere, he smiles. The smile turns into a laugh. Then I'm laughing with him. Tears are streaming down my eyes, I'm laughing so hard. It's crazy like that for a while, the two of us on the floor busting a gut. Then, like a cloud passing in front of the sun, it's over. We stand up.

Dad says, "Thanks, I needed that."

"Not a problem," I say.

"But don't ever do it again."

"Okay, but you scared the crap out of me first."

Dutch materializes out of the gray. He scratches at the door. I smile, knowing there's a steaming yard biscuit out there somewhere waiting for the POD commander's foot.

I open the door to let Dutch inside. For some reason he just sits there. The fog crawls up to the opening. Dad yells at me to close the door. Thin gray fingers curl around the jamb, then retreat. Without thinking I reach into the gray and grab Dutch's collar. The fog is on me. My arm starts to tingle. Dad screams, "Let go! Let go!" But I won't. I lock fingers around the leather strap. My hand is starting to disappear. Darkness clouds my eyes; then a split-second blinding flash explodes like a flare in my head. I pull one more time. Dutch gets up and walks inside.

Dad slams the door and locks it. "Are you okay?" he asks. He's looking at me like I just missed getting hit by a train.

I'm shaking. I look at my hand. Thankfully it's all there. A tingling sensation is moving up and down my arm, although it's fading fast. And the flash—that was freaky. But what would telling him accomplish, other than getting his panties in a bunch?

"I'm fine," I say, showing him my hand. "All five fingers, good as new."

He studies me. "You sure?"

"Yes."

"What were you thinking?"

I shrug. "It seemed like the thing to do."

The air has a strange smell, kind of orange and earthy. I take a whiff of my arm. The smell is there, weak but definitely there. I bend down and sniff Dutch. He's covered with it. Maybe this is the smell of the planet POD. A shiver sweeps over me.

Dad says, "You sure you're okay?"

"Other than feeling a strange desire to eat your liver, I'm fine."

He frowns. "All right, then. I'm going to make some breakfast. But no liver for you."

Dad walks into the kitchen. I peer out at the fog one more time. The sun is coming up, which brightens the stuff a shade or two. But it's still just as thick. The way it boils reminds me of tear gas I see in action movies, just before SWAT guys in battle gear storm the bus.

That gives me an idea I'd rather not have. Maybe it's time to storm the bus.

I head for the dining room, my arm still tingling.

- THE PIRATE MAKES A PLAN -

How could I be so stupid?

I stare at the note, as if by concentrating hard on the letters I can find Richie and stab a hole in his evil heart. *I have something you want.* Just the thought of him taking Cassie makes my blood boil. I need to get her back. Now that the sun is finally up I can do something about it.

Last night was spent under a truck on Level 4. No way was I going to sleep in the Volvo. I went down to Level 2 and fetched the horse blanket out of the drug dealer's car. Then I found this spot and tried to sleep, which was so not possible. It was the longest night of my life. The horse blanket isn't as warm as my sleeping bag, and it smells worse. I found some extra clothes and tried piling them on top of me, but they fell off every time I moved. No matter what I did, the cold seemed to find me. When I finally drifted off for a minute, the terrible screeching sound came. There was no way I could fall asleep after that, so I just shivered in the dark and thought about what I need to do and how I'm going to do it.

I crawl out from under the truck. My body aches from all the cold in my bones. I take a deep breath and look out at the new day. The air has a weird smell I can't quite figure out, like a mix between flowers and dirt. Better than gas and radiator fluid, that's for sure. There's a cold fog outside with a strange color, gray with smudges of yellowish blue. It's so thick I can't see the spaceballs, which is fine by me. In a way it's kind of fun to watch, how it moves and swirls just outside the walls of the garage without coming in. Maybe it's alien fog, or maybe it's just the way things are in a city that doesn't breathe anymore. There's a broom in the bed of the truck. I try an experiment. I stick the broom handle out into the fog. Right away the swirls wrap around it; then electricity flows up and down the handle like mini-lightning bolts. It freaks me out, so I drop the broom. The swirls follow it down. I hear it land, but I don't see where. Experiment over—definitely alien fog. But whatever the spaceballs are up to, I'm not going to waste time thinking about it.

They have their to-do list and I have mine.

First things first—*get the gun.* I sneak up to Level 6 and scope out the garbage can for a long time. After ninety-six minutes I'm pretty sure Richie isn't around. I sprint out, lift the top off the can, reach into the trash, grab the handle, and go. I dive under the nearest car and tick off eight minutes. All clear. I race to the Volvo to see if my treasures are still in the secret compartment by the spare tire. They are. I stuff them in my backpack and make my way down to Level 4. The briefcase seems heavier every time I pick it up.

I stop and listen at the entrance to each level. I've just reached the sign for Level 3 when I hear a sound. A kind of click behind me. I scurry under a car. On the way I bang my head on the muffler pipe, which is hanging by a wire. I wait twelve minutes, watching drops of my blood make small red dots on the oil-stained cement. Some of the dots join together to make something bigger. This isn't good.

I count another ninety seconds. Nothing. Whatever made that sound, it wasn't Richie.

Now I'm at the truck where I spent the night. I have a monster headache and a jagged gash over my left eye. I use the makeup mirror to see what's what. There's a loose flap of skin the size of a dime. It crosses into my left eyebrow. The wound is full of chunks of rust from the muffler. The little bit of my face that I can see is covered with dirt and streaked with blood. My hair used to be blond—now it's stringy and the color of mud. *Is that me?* I've gone from a zombie to a victim in one of Zack's slasher videos. I open the first-aid kit, pick out an alcohol pad, and press it against the wound. It burns like fire. My eyes water and I almost scream. Finally the pain shrinks to a dull throb. Then comes the bandage. Mom taught me to use a butterfly bandage on cuts like this one, so that's what I do. But the bandage doesn't stick to my eyebrow. I have to use a patch of gauze so big it covers my whole eye. I tape it down and hope for the best. One last look in the mirror. Ha! I do look like a pirate. I think about taking one of the azithro-something pills, but since I have no idea what they do, I go for the safer bet— aspirin. I shake two pills out of the bottle and swallow them dry. Headache or not, I'm good to go.

But go where? That's the zillion-dollar question. Do I knock on the door and say, "Yo, Richie, here's what you want, now give me what I want"? What will happen then? Will he give me my stuff? Will he give me Cassie and let us go back to our parking-garage world? Give me some food and water? Maybe invite me and Cassie to stay inside where it's warm and they make hamburgers for dinner and drink hot chocolate before bedtime? I shake my head. *Yeah, right!* More like it he'd take the gun and keep Cassie. That is, if Cassie is even alive. I have to face the facts. You can't trust people like Richie. Give them a gun and they grow a mean streak a mile wide. Like Mom used to say, they'll hurt you every chance they get.

And then there's Mr. Hendricks. If he bosses around people like Richie and Hacker, then meeting him must be like walking into a room full of angry bees.

Which means that I need to sneak in. But how? I heard Richie say they have guards at all the doors. I've seen some air vents that might work, but they're up too high. And even if I found one that I could crawl into, how would I take off the cover from the inside and get down to the floor? It works in movies, but this is real life. Real life has a way of tricking you into doing stupid stuff and then making you pay for it big-time.

I finger the patch on my eye, which makes me wonder: What would a pirate do? He'd find the darkest, scariest tunnel on the island, sneak past the stupid guards snoring next to the fire, and steal the treasure. I'm not sure if the door guards are stupid, but there is a dark, scary tunnel. There's a stairway marked *Utility Access—Hotel Employees Only on Level 1*. It's dark, definitely scary, and maybe there aren't any guards at all.

If I'm lucky.

- FLASH OF BRILLIANCE -

I'm feeling...weird.

It's been this way since I woke up this morning. I blame it on a dream that tortured me all night long—that the fog figured out how to open the doors, seeped into the house, and was oozing up the stairs. I finally managed to get back to sleep, but only after I repeated a thousand times that it is physically impossible for fog, unless it's made in Hollywood, to open doors.

We're finishing off the graham crackers for breakfast. Dad is going on about *My Side of the Mountain*, his favorite survival book as a kid. It actually sounds interesting, but I can't concentrate. That weird feeling is getting stronger by the second. It's like I'm on that first slow ride up a roller coaster. Now I'm almost at the very top, where the car hovers in that weightless place just before you start to fall and gravity tries to squeeze your heart through your eyeballs. It's making me restless, on edge.

Dad stops mid-sentence and says, "Are you okay?"

I nod but it's a barefaced lie. My right hand is tingling.

He waits a beat, stands up, carries his plate into the kitchen.

The tingling moves in waves from fingertip to elbow. It's exactly like yesterday when I reached out into the fog. Same arm, same place. The graham cracker slides from my fingers. Dad has his back to me—he's putting his plate in the cupboard.

There's a moment of blackness, like a shutter clicking in front of a camera lens.

Then bam! Another blinding flash. My body shudders. A few seconds later and I'm fine. The almost-falling sensation is gone. If it weren't so creepy, I'd say I feel pretty damn good.

Dad walks back to the table. "What's up with the face?" he says, giving me a sideways look.

"What face is that?"

"The one you have when you're trying not to smile."

I hold the cracker in my right hand and admire it as if it's a work of art.

"Dad, without question, this is the best breakfast you ever made."

I'm sitting in the Amanda chair, gazing out into the swirling soup. It's thicker than ever. It almost looks angry. If the POD commander stood two inches from the glass, I wouldn't be able to see him—or her. The grayness is so complete that I have to wonder, is anything left? Are all the fences and playground slides and porta-potties and road signs dissolved and we're the last people in the last man-made structure on the planet, a planet soon to be renamed POD II?

Dad, still unnerved about my "encounter" yesterday, is checking up on me every fifteen minutes or so. The binoculars are in my lap. It's a Dad decoy. I have no hope of seeing Amanda, or anything else beyond the window. All I'm really doing is trying to figure out what's going on. I've had no more episodes since this morning. I suppose that's a good thing. I've come close to telling Dad about it, but at the last second a voice in my head says that it's probably not a good idea. So I hold off for now. But if I were to tell him, I would have only one thing to say.

Of all the stupid stuff I've done or said since the PODs arrived, reaching out into that fog ranks number one—by a mile.

- OUT OF THE FRYING PAN -

Here's my plan.

Part 1: Get In.
Hide pepper spray in right hand.
Knock on door.
When guard opens door, ask for Richie.
Walk in and pretend to trip on floor.
Pretend to cry (make it look good).
When guard bends down to see what's wrong, zap him in face with
>pepper spray.

Run like crazy.
Hide.

Part 2: Steal Treasure.
Find the treasure (Cassie).
Hide until everyone is asleep.
Steal treasure.
Part 3: Get Out.
Use escape route.
Hide in cave until coast is clear.
Live in parking garage until food runs out or spaceball drivers finally
>attack.

Of course there are problems with the plan. Like, what if I can't find any place to hide? Or I hide and they find me? Or I miss with the pepper spray? Or I run out of food before I find Cassie? Or I can't find Cassie, or my escape route is blocked? All sorts of things can go wrong. I've learned that when you make a plan, it's a good idea to have a backup plan handy in case the first one doesn't work. I have one of those, too. Take Richie up on his trade. If he wants the gun that much, he can have it. All I care about right now is getting Cassie back.

I hike back to the cave and stash half the water and the rest of the beef jerky. Then, back at Level 1 I load my backpack with the tools I might need: two screwdrivers, the makeup mirror (for seeing around corners), the busted Swiss army knife, white tape from the first-aid kit, three PowerBars, some wire from a coat hanger, and a half bottle of water. I smear my face, even my eye patch, with streaks of engine oil. I tie a black scarf around my head and jam the glow sticks into my waistband. The metal case gets stuffed up under the back-seat cushion of the crappiest car in the whole garage—Mom's '78 Nova. No one will find it there. I review the plan in my head, then take a final look around my world.

Outside there's still the swirling yellowish blue fog. If I stare long enough, sometimes I see small flashes of light inside, like bug zappers on a hot summer night. It's so thick it's like the rest of the world isn't there. A part of me wonders why it doesn't come into the parking garage. The other part of me wonders why it would want to. Wrecked cars, broken glass, stuffed animals with missing parts, clothing that's too big or too small, old newspapers, and all the other assorted pieces of lives that scared people in a hurry left behind. Oh, and one long, dark stain. A heaviness leaks into my bones. It could be the fog—or maybe it's something else.

But I don't have time for this kind of thinking. I shake my brain until it clears. Take a deep breath. Shoulders back. Okay.

I head for the stairs.

Three knocks on the door. No one answers. I knock again. Same thing. I test the doorknob. Locked. I pull on the door. It seems to move a little, so I pull again, harder. It swings open, almost knocking me over. Maybe the latch was full of dust or something was wedged in the doorway. Maybe it's a trap. And maybe, just maybe, a piece of luck floated my way for once. I don't see anyone inside.

Whatever the reason, I put the pepper spray in my pocket and walk in.

Light from outside spills into a room that isn't much bigger than the toolshed back home. There's two gray electrical boxes on the wall with useless yellow-and-black stickers reading *Danger—High Voltage*, a calendar still stuck on January showing a guy doing some upside-down stunt on a snowboard, a folded-up stepladder in the corner. There's an air-conditioning vent above the ladder—it's covered with dusty cobwebs. Moving to the right, there's a metal desk, a metal chair with a dark sweater hanging over the back, a small calculator, a desk lamp, a Starbucks coffee cup, a mop, and two buckets. And two more feet to the right, another door. There's an awful rotting sour smell I can't quite figure out. I know it's not a bloater, though. That smell I'll never forget.

The moment of truth.

I tiptoe to the other door and wrap my fingers around the handle. It turns. I pull a little; the door opens a crack. And squeaks. I close the door. Another squeak, loud enough for someone to hear. I run to the outside door, which is still open, and wait. My heart is pogo-sticking against my chest. I'm ready to run like a rabbit if that inside door opens. I set my brain clock to five minutes. Nothing. I close the outside door, test it to make sure it still opens. It sticks a little but works. Okay. Escape route secure. Now the room is totally black. I reach for one of the glow sticks, then stop. Not yet; need to save those. I close my one good eye and picture the room. I put my hands out in front of me and zombie-walk until I touch the opposite wall, move slowly to my right, touch the desk, the lamp, the coffee cup. It falls to the floor with a soft thump and a splash. Now I know where the smell is coming from. I wait a couple of heartbeats, then feel my way along the wall to the door handle. Turn, pull, squeak, wait. Pull, squeak, wait. One more pull. I fit my head through the opening. More black, more silence. I step through the space and into...

A hall, I think. Or at least it *feels* like a hall. I measure the width of the space with steps. I count twenty from one side to the other, and who knows how long it is. I'm about to close the door when I freeze. It's locked from the hall side. There's no un-lock button on the other side of the handle. If I close this door, which is one of those un-smashable metal fire doors, then there goes my escape route. Good-bye to Part 3 of the plan. *Stupid, stupid, stupid!* I take off my pack, fumble around for the tape, tear off a piece, and stick it over the latch. Note to self: *Don't be stupid.*

Now for Part 2—find the treasure.

As I move down the hall I remember something. One night Mom and I were sitting on the couch watching TV when I saw a mouse run under Zack's chair. We chased the mouse, but it got away. The next day I saw another mouse (or maybe the same mouse) in the kitchen, and we couldn't catch that one either. So all of a sudden we had this big problem. Mom wanted to set mousetraps, but Zack said no, use poison. After a couple of weeks, no more mice. And two weeks later our neighbor's cat died. The vet told them it was because she ate poisoned mice. Zack told Mom that if a cat is so stupid it eats poisoned mice, it deserves to die. And that, Mom told me while we were driving through a thunderstorm in Colorado, is when she started making her escape plan. That and the time he showed her a gun and said it had a bullet with her name on it if she ever tried to run away. Anyway, the point of this is that I learned mice stay close to the walls when they move through a room. So that's how I move down this hallway in the dark—close to the wall and quiet as a mouse.

There are five more doors along the way, all locked. I touch a fire extinguisher on the wall next to door three and almost knock over a garbage can between doors four and five. Smooth, Megs. I reach the end of the hall and it takes a left turn. There's a thin sliver of light in the distance. Another door? As I get closer I hear voices. People talking. Conversations! Something that should seem as normal as getting out of bed, but gives me a chill instead. I touch the door, reach around for the handle.

It's locked. There's an air vent above the door. Filtered light and pieces of conversations are leaking in from the other side. The vent is too high for me to look through, but I have an idea—the ladder from the utility room. I walk back and get the ladder, being careful not kick the garbage can or bang it against the walls.

Back at the door now, I open the ladder and climb all the way to the top. It's a little shaky, so I use the door for balance. Looking through the vent, I can see three steps leading up to a big room with a high ceiling and lots of windows. Probably the hotel lobby. A shiny wooden counter is at the far side of the room with paintings behind it and a big sign on the wall saying HOTEL EXCELSIOR. Black rugs dot the white floor and there's a row of tall windows on one side of the counter. With the fog outside the windows it looks like this is a hotel in the clouds. On the other side of the counter is a door with smoky dark glass. There's painted writing on the glass that reads *Misty's Restaurant*.

I count twenty people, but there's probably more. Some are sitting in lounge chairs reading magazines, some walking around, some in corners talking, but most are standing in a long line that leads to I don't know where. There are three kids, a boy and two girls, standing in the line next to a woman. Her eyes have the glassy look of a dead fish. The boy is around my age; the girls are younger, red-haired twins. The boy has a cell phone and he's pretending to talk with the aliens. He's telling them to beam up his stupid ugly sisters. This bugs the twins, who keep trying to take the phone. The woman wakes from her trance long enough to grab the boy's arm and whisper something in his ear. Whatever it is, he doesn't pay attention because the next thing I know the woman reaches down, snatches the phone out of his hand, and snaps it in half. She gives one half to each of the twins. The boy stares at her, his mouth swinging open like a broken trapdoor.

My eyes move on to more important things. There are three men in the room. Hacker is standing to the right of the restaurant door, cleaning a gun with his shirtsleeve. After every cough he spits into the pot of the plant beside him. The guy on the other side of the door is slouched in a chair. I'm pretty sure a gun is poking out the top of his sweatpants. It looks like he's sleeping, but every once in a while his head turns a little, just enough to see it's Black Beard. And he's definitely not sleeping. The third guard is standing at the top of the stairs, no more than six feet from where I'm balancing on a shaky ladder. I can't see his face because he's wearing a hood and turned the wrong way. But I see his boots.

Snakeskin.

A woman walks up to Richie. Her sad eyes are ringed with shadows and she slides one foot as she walks. She's holding a baby wrapped loosely in a blue blanket. The baby's face is bright red and he's taking short, raspy breaths. The woman asks Richie if she can see the man in charge right away, it's an emergency. He ignores her. There's a woman in the background, sitting on a couch. She was reading a magazine. Now she's focused on this conversation.

The mother says, "Please. My baby, he needs something for his fever."

Richie says, "You think I care about that?" He points to the end of the line. "No cuts, lady. Go wait your turn like everyone else."

The people in the line don't pay any attention. They keep inching forward. But the woman in the background is heading this way. She's short and thin and probably doesn't weigh much more than me. But the way she moves, light and smooth like a dancer, reminds me of one of my favorite people—Aunt Janet. Aunt Janet was a gymnast in high school and can still do a back flip anytime she wants.

The mother stands there, frozen. Her shoulders start shaking. She puts her head down, turns away.

Aunt Janet says to her, "Stop. Wait right there." Then she says to Richie, "What's your problem? Can't you see this is a medical emergency?"

Richie, turning to face her, says, "I can see just fine."

She says, "I'm tired of the way you treat people."

Richie says, "That a fact?"

She says, "Just because you have—"

Richie's hand slides into his pocket, pulls out the knife, flips it open, points the tip at Aunt Janet's head. The whole thing happened in less than three seconds.

He says, "Just because I have this?"

Aunt Janet stops talking. She stares up at the blade six inches from her throat.

Richie says, "Listen close, 'cause I'm not going to say this again." The knife starts weaving slow like syrup through his fingers. "I don't care if the baby's head is about to explode like a piñata, all right? I don't care if its hair is on fire or killer bees are flying out its ass. It waits in line like everyone else."

Aunt Janet says, "The baby is a boy. Not an 'it.'"

The knife stops moving. Richie says, "Looks like a worm to me."

The mother says, "Please...I...I can wait in line."

Aunt Janet, not looking at the knife anymore but straight into that hood, says, "People like you shouldn't be allowed to crawl out from under rocks."

Richie says, "And you're not worth the mess."

His hand moves in a blur. I blink my eyes. The knife is gone.

The mother moves to the end of the line.

Aunt Janet walks back to the couch, her body stiff like she's frozen from the waist up, and sits. She picks up the magazine, but her eyes stay locked on Richie.

Richie starts whistling a snappy tune, those snakeskin boots tapping to the beat.

- THE SIGHTING -

It's who-knows-what o'clock in the afternoon. I'm lying on my bed watching this amazing show: Dutch licking his balls. It's been going on for at least half an hour. His nut sack should be the cleanest thing in the house by now. I think it's something he does to calm his nerves—the canine version of meditation. Close my eyes and it sounds like waves lapping against the shore.

Thinking about meditation gets me thinking about Mom and her yoga classes. Yoga is one of her favorite things to do. Which leads me to a stupid fight we had last month. She needed the Camry for yoga class and I needed it to meet Alex for a movie at the mall. I asked her if she could miss a class, just this once. She said no—"especially not today." There was something strange in the way she said it—like that class on that day was a matter of life and death. She'd been acting a little nervous and teary, so I knew it was a pointless battle. But I yelled something stupid anyway, like, "It's only freaking stretching class, you can do that at home!" I wound up taking the bus and missing the first twenty minutes of the movie. I didn't talk to her for three days. And the movie sucked.

That gets me thinking about Alex and how he's not the best movie buddy because popcorn—a food he can't resist—turns him into a gas factory. A noxious cloud starts to form within minutes of his first mouthful and stays with him the whole time. But that's good in a way since I'm pretty much immune. People within a four-seat radius usually move, which guarantees that I get a clear shot of the movie and an armrest all to myself.

Anyway, in the middle of this licking and nostalgia I have an episode. It's over in five seconds. The tingling doesn't bother me, but that moment of blackness—something about it gives me the willies. But after the flash, now *there's* a feeling I could get used to. I'm trying to hold on to that when I notice my bedroom is getting lighter—fast. The fog, a constant lurking presence for two days, is finally leaving. Actually, dissolving is a better word, like salt in hot water after a couple of stirs. All those freaky gray swirls with the mini-lightning bolts—gone in less than a minute. If I hadn't looked up I would have missed it. The sun is shining in a cloudless blue, POD-stained sky. But when I think about it, the salt isn't really gone, right? You can't see it, but you can taste it. So I'm wondering if the POD commander finally decided, *Hey, it's time to pick up a spoon and stir the cup.*

Then it hits me—no fog, so I can see across the street! I jump out of bed and sprint downstairs.

Amanda is at the window, waiting for me. Her hair is pulled back in a tight ponytail, and she's wearing the same purple UW sweatshirt, only it looks different, like it's two sizes bigger. For just a second I wonder if my clothes, which feel a little saggy, look like that on me. She presses her message to the window.

Amanda: IM 15 2day

Her birthday is close to mine. Very cool. What else do we have in common? The fog is gone and now this. I'm feeling some good karma despite the crashed bike in the cul-de-sac and the POD commander above her apartment taking notes. I post my reply.

Me: happy bday 2U.

She smiles, but the smile is missing something—like, the happy part? Then she blows me a kiss...and leaves! Her message is still up. Eventually it falls. I wait.

And wait.

And wait.

And wait.

She doesn't come back. All those days with the fog, all that time wondering if I'll ever see her again, and then this? "IM 15 2day"! She blew me a kiss, sure, but what the hell? It's her birthday! Then I think, *Oh, yeah, it's her birthday*—like when Dad forgot about my birthday and I sat in the Camry and thought about backing it out of the garage while he counted food packets in the kitchen. Now I understand her smile.

I'm restless and jittery so I wander the house, opening and closing doors, sliding from room to room like the ghost that I am. Dad is asleep and snoring on the couch in the living room. Dutch is finished meditating. He's curled up on the rug by my bed. The bathrooms are historic relics with useless porcelain thrones. The linen closet has towels folded in perfect rectangles and stacked in parallel, color-coordinated columns, waiting for showers that will never be. The house is quiet and calm except for the snoring man. A warm spring sun is streaming in through windows and skylights.

I should feel at peace, but I don't. My skin crawls, like there's a nest of earwigs under my skin. It's quiet, yeah, but like they say in the movies right before the bog monster attacks, maybe it's a little *too* quiet. So I keep on moving. As I walk I notice a hole in my left sock. One of my toenails is poking through. If Alex saw this he'd say, "Dude, bust out the clippers before you kill someone."

We're running out of stuff. Little things like Q-tips and roll-on deodorant. And big things, like toilet paper today, and yesterday when we used up the last of the fuel for the camping stove. Now if we want hot food we'll have to heat it in the fireplace using furniture for wood. Dad put the sledgehammer to the bed frame and dresser in the guestroom. The pieces are stacked up in the living room, ready to go.

I open the pantry door and—*what the hell?* My eyes bug out, not because of how little is left, but because of how it *looks*. There are four shelves, and each shelf has one, two, three, yup, four cans, except the bottom shelf, which has two cans, one small jar of pickled artichoke hearts, and a plastic container of pizza sauce. Four envelopes of powdered milk lean at an angle against the back wall. The containers are in the exact geographical center of each shelf, lined up tallest to shortest, like little marines at the can academy. There's another layer of order here, too, but it takes me few moments to figure it out. The labels are all rotated just a touch, like maybe ten degrees, clockwise. Then I spot a sheet of notebook paper taped to the inside of the door. It has rows and columns of neatly written entries detailing dates and quantities used down to the quarter-ounce.

This isn't a pantry anymore, it's a food shrine.

The urge is irresistible. I switch a can of kidney beans on the left side of the top shelf with a smaller can of creamed corn in a middle position on the bottom shelf. I rotate the pizza sauce counterclockwise ten degrees, then close the door and move on.

The kitchen is a tale of two stories. We used to have a relatively "normal" kitchen. A little on the messy side, but clean enough. Sometimes we'd leave dishes in the sink from one meal to the next. Now it literally shines. I see my distorted reflection in the metal sink. The countertops are bare and white. I slide my hand along the top of the center island. Smooth as polished stone. No crumbs, no dust. My fingers have a faint scent of disinfectant.

Water is the other story here. I thought we had more. A lot more, actually. The miscellaneous containers and bins are empty. There are eight baggies left; the others leaked. Someone, a.k.a. me, blew it by not sealing them well enough. But the bathtub is full. Dad figures if we're careful that should last us at least a month, maybe two. We had a déjà vu moment about that, with me saying, That's great, we'll have water but no food.

He said, We've been careless about consuming our resources and that has to stop.

I said, Why bother?

He said, Because we have to.

I said, What's the point?

He said, Because the alternative is unacceptable.

Blah, blah, blah.

And then there's the ball-licker. That's a train wreck waiting to happen. Dutch's food bag is two days from bingo. Then what? We've been letting him out on the long rope, hoping he'll drink from the swamp. But he doesn't understand the concept. From his perspective, water magically appears in the empty bowl on the rubber mat. He nudges it with his nose, stares at me with those liquid brown eyes, then sits in the dead grass by the door and waits for the magic to happen. But Dad says he doesn't get any more water, not even from the toilet, which is essentially empty. He says when "the dog" gets thirsty enough he'll figure out what to do. Right. And he'll start catching rabbits too, maybe even bring us a squirrel.

I stand by the patio door and squint out into the sun. The birds are chirping like crazy, flying around, chasing each other, enjoying their freedom. I figure the hell with it and open the door. Warm air flows in, maybe somewhere in the low sixties. Definitely nice for this time of year. It's tempting to just step outside, feel grass beneath my feet...

I take a deep, grateful breath. I'm tired of being cooped up in a house with two adult males and a dog, all of whom need showers and deodorant. The air smells good. Not perfect—there's still an alien fog aftertaste, but it's just barely there. I mean, if I didn't know about the fog and took a whiff, I'd wonder if a thunderstorm passed through.

There's movement in the tall bushes bordering our yard. Whatever it is, it's really shaking the branches. I'm thinking a big dog, like a Great Dane, or a Shetland pony. Then it walks out onto the grass and I can't believe what I'm seeing. A deer—a full-grown, honest-to-God, Bambi-shaped deer. And then another one comes out, bigger and with horns—excuse me, antlers. They're munching on branches, chewing a cud, whatever it is they do. Two deer close enough for me to see the hair in their noses. This is an absolute first in our neighborhood. I want to yell to Dad, but for some bizarre reason I'm afraid I'll scare them. So I watch the happy couple, ears twitching in the sun, slowly graze their way up around the swamp and over a small hill and disappear. A short while later, looking through the binoculars, I spot them walking into the shadow of a POD.

On that note I hear a cough and a groan from the living room. Dad's waking up. Good. We have something to talk about.

He's sitting on the couch, rubbing his eyes and yawning when I come in. I'm still not used to seeing all that hair on his face. I have a pathetic dusting of teen fuzz. He's turning into the Beardman from Alcatraz.

I sit on the coffee table facing him and say, "Have a nice nap?"

"Not really. This couch is bad for my back."

"You notice anything different?"

He looks around. His eyes go from bleary to focused. "The fog is gone."

"Score one for the dadster."

"When did that happen?"

I look at my wrist where a watch used to be. "Uh, two thirty-seven?"

He frowns.

"About an hour ago," I say. "It just...dissolved."

I get a nod, like that makes perfect sense. Then he says, with a flash of panic, "What's that smell? Is the door open?"

"For the past half-hour," I say. "The BO in here is more toxic than alien death fog."

Dad gets up. I follow him into the family room. He stands in front of the door, takes a careful whiff. "Ozone," he says.

"That's the fog smell?"

"It happens when unstable free oxygen molecules, or two O's, recombine with molecular oxygen, or O_2, to make ozone, which is O_3."

"Wow. I just love it when you talk chemistry to me. I wish you'd do it more."

Still looking out the door, he says, "So what have you been up to?"

He's using a "wink-wink" tone that means he wants to know if I communicated with my special friend. That's a place I don't go with him.

"Guess what I saw while you were snoring?" Asking this question gives me a fluttery feeling, like it's better left unasked. I don't know why.

"Mr. Conrad?"

"Nope."

"Somebody get zapped?"

"Nope."

"I'm running out of options here." He snaps his fingers. "I know! The fog cleared and you saw Elvis!"

"Even more amazing," I say, and point to the field. "Two deer, right there. They walked up and over the hill."

"Deer? In our back yard?"

"Bambi and her stud."

"That close?"

"Yup. Not ten feet from where we're standing."

He shakes his head, blows out a disappointed sigh. "That's too bad."

"Why?" I ask, wondering how this can possibly be a bad thing.

"One of those deer could feed us for a month."

And there you have it, folks. I see Bambi. He sees deer cutlets frying in a pan.

That's why I didn't want to tell him.

- THE INTRODUCTION -

I'm standing on the ladder and spying through a dusty vent with my good eye. My other eye, the one with the patch, sends spikes of white-hot pain stabbing into my head every time I touch it or I bump it by accident. Which is exactly what happens every time my legs cramp from standing on tiptoe. This is my second day in the hotel and I have no idea where Cassie is, or even if she's alive. Richie went into the restaurant about an hour ago. He's probably having a sandwich and a beer.

Mom would scream like a boiling monkey if she knew what I was doing and why, but here I am anyway. She didn't call me Crazy Megs for nothing. I'll give it one more day, just one, then it's back to the garage for me. Back to the smashed-up cars and moldy crumbs and stinking bloaters.

The door to the restaurant opens. Two men walk into the lobby, one behind the other. The first one is Richie. Still wearing the hoodie. I wonder what's up with that. From what I can see, he looks as mean as ever. The other man I've never seen before. He's at least a head taller than Richie and has wide shoulders and a big, square face. While everyone else looks ratty and tired, he seems like he's fresh out of the shower with his black hair slicked back. He's wearing tan slacks, a white shirt, and a blue sport jacket. There's some kind of logo on the jacket so maybe it's a uniform. He could be a soap opera star, or the ex-con who sold Mom our piece-of-crap Nova. Whoever he is, when he walks into the center of the lobby the rooms falls so quiet you could hear a mouse breathe.

He raises his arm and says, "I apologize, but certain unfortunate events require that I intrude on your day. I've been informed that two bottles of medicinal alcohol and some aspirin were stolen from one of my staff. This is truly disappointing. Those items were being used to improve the comfort of guests in need. When someone steals from one of us, they steal from all of us."

He moves in a slow circle while he talks, pausing to look at individual faces, like he's in a wax museum and they're the statues on display. Sometimes he smiles, sometimes he doesn't. Once or twice when his jacket opens I see a flash of brown under his arm. I'm thinking it's a holster and gun.

"Only one person is in charge of who gets what and when, and that person is me. There are *zero exceptions* to this rule." His voice picks up an edge that startles me. I bump my bad eye and instantly feel jolts of scorching pain. My good eye starts to water.

The man takes a deep breath, lets it out slow, and says, "As director of security in this hotel, it's my job to maintain safety and order. We must catch this thief and deal swiftly with the problem. I'm offering one bottle of water and five cigarettes to the person who turns the thief in. Your cooperation will be strictly confidential. If I don't have an answer by this time tomorrow morning we will skip a water day. I assure you that would be very bad for the folks up on floor ten. If I don't have an answer in two days, well—we don't want to see that happen, do we, Mr. Smith?" He turns to Richie.

Richie, underneath that hood, smiles like a wolf and says, "No, sir, Mr. Hendricks. We sure don't."

"Good. Now if you will all excuse me, I need to get back my appointments. Mrs. Solomon is having problems with her ankles."

Mr. Hendricks raises his arm and waves to the group like this is no big deal, but everyone knows it is. I see that flash of brown again. Definitely a holster and gun. He walks into the restaurant and closes the door.

It takes a few moments for air to come back into the room, a few more minutes for people to start whispering and nodding in clumps of two or three. Richie and Hacker return to their posts. A line forms in front of me. They used to talk. Now they just stare straight ahead, silent and still.

I look across the lobby and out the windows. It's a sunny day.

No one seems to notice except me. The fog is gone.

DAY 19: PROSSER, WASHINGTON

- FINAL ANSWER -

I'm sitting at my post in front of the living room window, binoculars in hand, waiting for her to grace me with a visit. I'm like Dutch in the old days. He'd wait right here, muzzle resting on the windowsill, for me to come home from school. In fact, there's a permanent drool stain in the wood. I'm pathetic, I know, but what can I say? It's not like this place is a hub of activity. I already checked out the pantry. The cans are back in their appropriate rows, minus the niblet corn and the pickled artichokes we had for breakfast this morning.

A thought comes to me, and it isn't the first time for this one. Why is the bike still there?

I mean, the POD commander deleted everything else—cars, trucks, planes, you name it. But the bike—it's still there. Is it some kind of reminder, to make sure I don't forget who's in charge? If so, then it's working like a freaking stroke of genius. I can't look out this window without seeing Jamie disappear, not ten steps from where I'm sitting. But then a hairy pair of arms kept me from helping her. Because of him I'll be seeing Jamie, her wide-eyed mix of hope and fear and—

"You up for some Scrabble?"

Speaking of Pod-Zilla, here he is, stomping into the living room.

Torturing him with triple word scores is fun but not high on my list right now. I have something better to do. Like looking at this cul-de-sac, at the bike that's always there, the POD that never moves or sleeps, the girl who should be in the window but isn't. So instead of saying yes, I set down the binoculars and say, "What happens when our food runs out?"

"Wow. I wasn't expecting that." He sits on the floor facing me, leans back on his elbows.

"So?" I say. "What's your plan?"

"It's a complicated question."

"No. Either you have a plan or you don't. You always have a plan."

He says, "Okay, you're right. I have a plan. But it's...evolving. I'd rather not talk about it now."

"You'd rather play Scrabble?"

"Yes."

"Than talk about our future?"

"Scrabble is more fun."

"There you go again, Dad, avoiding the harsh realities of life."

He smiles.

"You want to know what I think?"

"Always," he says.

"Okay. The way I see it, there are only two choices."

This gets the silent nod. I *hate* the silent nod.

I say, "One, we starve to death, or two, we get deleted."

"Which do you pick?"

"First, a question: Does starvation hurt?"

"For a while," he says. "But I've heard that once you get past the point where the organs shut down, it's painless. Even peaceful."

"Like drowning?"

"The romanticized version, yes."

He transitions from sitting to lying down, head propped on his fingers, staring up at the ceiling. We have a fine collection of cobwebs up there. Now that Dad has seen them, I expect they'll be gone by tomorrow. At this moment, when I should be contemplating the moral implication of choosing death by POD or death by starvation, I realize I don't even know what day it is—Monday, Wednesday, Sunday? Then again, so what? Time is no longer measured in units, it's just the indefinite space between waking and sleeping. Sooner or later that won't matter because—

"So?" he says.

I say, "Uh, deleted. Definitely the way to go."

"Final answer?"

It sounds like he was thinking door number two and I went for door number one. "Deleted. Final answer."

"Why?"

"Very quick, probably painless, and maybe we're not really killed. Maybe we're beamed somewhere."

"Like heaven?"

"I'm not ruling it out. But it could be another planet, or another dimension—like a flowery meadow where singing butterflies ride on the backs of unicorns."

He says, "Maybe it's a place where you're forced to work in alien mines deep below the surface of some barren asteroid, digging with blistered fingers for toxic fuel. Or maybe you're kept in feed lots, like those cows we pass on the way to Seattle."

No one kills a buzz like Dad. "Whatever," I say. "I go with the freaking unicorns."

He stands up. When I say "freaking" he usually leaves the room. For him it's the verbal equivalent of a fart. But this conversation needs closure, so I ask, "Which do you choose?"

He rubs the hair on his face and says, "I defer my vote to a later date. There may be other options."

"Avoiding reality again?"

"It's my prerogative as the elder statesman."

"Well, you better hurry," I say, picking up the binoculars and turning toward the window. "We're running out of kidney beans."

Later that night a howling wind comes up. This seems to happen a lot, way more than in the pre-POD world. Tonight it happens well after I've gone to bed, rattling the window and shaking me out of a deep, dreamless sleep. I try going back to that place, where emptiness actually feels good, but I can't. I'm thirsty. I need a drink of water, just a sip, something to help peel my tongue from the roof of my mouth. Dad will never know. I slip out of bed. Dutch thumps his tail twice and goes back to sleep.

As I feel my way down the stairs, I notice a flickering light from somewhere below. Did someone forget to pinch out a candle?

Fire Marshal Dad wouldn't approve! Down a few more steps and I hear a sound. Something rhythmic and steady, mixed in with a dose of heavy breathing. Is that *him?*

I'm at the bottom of the steps, staying on the carpet as I creep down the hall toward the kitchen. When I reach the corner I have a view of the patio door. I see Dad's reflection in the dark glass. He's in the kitchen, a burning candle on the counter beside him. There's also a white spray bottle and what looks like a glass of water. He rubs the counter with a rag, his hand moving in slow, meticulous circles. He's really leaning into it, concentrating, bald patch down, like there's some stain that just won't come out. After a few more rubs he picks up the spray bottle, squirts a few blasts at another spot, then goes back to work. Then he takes a spoon, dips it in the glass, and drizzles it over the spot. He rubs that down with a different rag. Then he picks up the spray bottle, moves slightly to the right...

I've seen enough. I turn around and slip back to my room.

With the door closed and absolute darkness enveloping me, I contemplate this new rip in the fabric of my life. And Dutch starts licking his balls. Perfect.

DAY 19: LOS ANGELES, CALIFORNIA

- THE WHISPERING WOMEN -

I think my eye is infected. It's gone from sore when I touch it, to a steady throbbing pain no matter what. I feel a whopper of a headache coming on, too. I can't do this ladder thing anymore. I need to find Cassie before it's too late, for her and for me. There are two ways I can do that. One is to walk right in and tell Richie that I'll give him the gun if he'll give me Cassie. The other way is a lot harder and I start sweating just thinking about it, but if it means avoiding Richie and Mr. Hendricks, then I'm ready to try.

I fold up the ladder and lug it back to the utility room. That's where I slept for the past two nights. It was shivering cold, but luckily whoever worked there left a sweatshirt behind, so I didn't need to sleep in a car. I got scared on the second night because I heard noises and it was so dark, darker than the Volvo trunk even, that I broke down and used a glow stick. It died this morning, so now there's only three left. That was stupid.

I count doors as I walk and think about the facts: There are three guards I've seen— Richie, Hacker, and Black Beard. They all have guns. They take turns guarding the doors, even at night when everybody is sleeping. I'm not sure what they're guarding and why, because no one can use the outside entrance—the Spaceballs make sure that doesn't happen. The green door that leads to the parking garage is used only when someone picks up a bucket and goes out to the sewer. The only other way in that I know about is my secret way—the utility room.

There's a door to the stairway that goes up to the tenth floor. I can't see it from the vent, but I hear it opening and closing all day long. I don't think there's a guard. But there are at least three more guards on the tenth floor. I heard Richie talk about "Jamie and Myles and that worthless Russian." I've seen Hacker go up there, too. That makes six total, not including Mr. Hendricks.

I reach the seventh door on the left, push it open. The tape is still over the latch. I slip into the utility room, close the door behind me, work my way to the outside door, and open it a crack. There's just enough light outside for me to see what I'm doing.

I take the tools I need out of the backpack and stuff them in my pockets: broken knife, pepper spray, makeup mirror, wire and tape, screwdriver, PowerBars, and the last three glow sticks. I put the baggie of weed in the top middle drawer of the desk and hide my backpack in one of the buckets. Pockets bulging, I climb the ladder to the air-conditioning vent, then use my screwdriver to twist out the screws. I pull back the vent cover. It's a tight fit, but without the backpack I'll manage okay.

I crawl like a worm into the vent.

Right away all the horror movies I've ever seen flood into my head. I fire up a glow stick and clamp it between my teeth as I slide on my belly, elbows and arms out in front. It's a small and dusty tunnel made of metal that echoes when I bump my head on the roof, which is every five seconds. Spiderwebs stick to my face and hair and lips, and disgusting brown things crunch under my elbows. I'm pretty sure they're mouse turds.

But that isn't the worst part. As I wiggle my way down this long, narrow tunnel with branches that to lead to dark and scary places, I realize that there isn't enough room to turn around. To get out I'll have to crawl backwards, which means I can't see where I'm going. If the glow sticks run out and I get lost, I'll be spider food for sure. The next person to crawl through this tunnel (like that will ever happen!) would find the dried-up skeleton of a twelve-year-old girl with a plastic stick clamped between her bony teeth and a bandage over her empty right eye socket.

My first turn is at a T that goes either left or right. I pick right because it feels like I'm over the hall and heading toward the door with the vent. That's probably the best place to start. But before making the turn I get an idea. I take out the tape and mark this spot with a small V. Between these markers and my trail in the dust, I should be able find my way back to the utility room.

I make two wasted turns that end with vents overlooking dark, silent rooms. I wait and listen, but nothing seems to be going on. So I crawl backwards, find my markers, and keep moving down what I now call the LTT, which means Long Tunnel of Tortures. I come to a branch that goes left. There's a light at the end. I bust through a wall of spiderwebs to check it out.

It's the hotel lobby, but this time I'm at floor level and facing a wall with paintings and mirrors. The counter is to my right instead of straight across. There's a plant in front of the vent, so I can't see a whole lot, but I see enough. It feels good to breathe air that isn't flavored with dried mouse turds and to look out at an open space. I take a nibble from a PowerBar and settle in for a long afternoon of watching. I smile because, for right now at least, I know what it feels like to be a mouse in a wall.

People walk by, but it's not very often and I hear only bits of the conversation as they pass. It takes forever, but I manage to learn a few things.

Two women are angry because today was supposed to be a water day, but thanks to the thief they don't get any. "The longer this goes on, the worse it's going to get for all of us," the second woman says. Then the first woman says, "I stayed at this hotel before, and Mr. Hendricks was nice then. But now all this power has gone to his head—you can never tell when these ex-cop security types are going to snap. Someone better find this thief, and fast."

A teenage girl tells her friend that the worst part of all this is she still looks fat. Her friend says, "Like, no duh, this is, like, the worst vacation *ever*."

A woman with a cane tells another woman that she's worried about her husband because there's a flu going around. The men are dropping like flies locked up on the tenth floor like that. The other woman, who's a lot younger, says she heard that one of the guards threw two bodies out the window last night. One of bodies was still breathing.

All this watching on my belly gives me a headache the size of France. My eyelids are hanging like they're weighted with lead.

Thank goodness I have to pee; otherwise I'd fall asleep and probably snore like a moose. So I'm trying to figure out if I can hold it when two women actually sit on the floor next to the plant. One I'm able to see—it's the woman with the sick baby. The baby is asleep on her lap. The other woman is blocked by the plant. All I see are her feet. But when she whispers, "Mary, you can trust me, whatever it is," I recognize the voice right away. It's Aunt Janet.

Mary says, "I'm the one they're looking for."

Aunt Janet says, "*You?* How?"

Mary says, "One of the guards was in the stairwell with the girl who worked at the front desk—the one with the pierced nose. I think he gives her supplies in exchange for you-know-what. Anyway, they were doing it like crazy behind the stairs. I see his pants on the floor, so I open the door, sneak in, and go through the pockets. I found a bottle of aspirin and two of those bottles from the mini-bar."

"What was in the bottles?"

"Vodka and whiskey."

"Which guard?"

Mary says, "The one with the knife who kept telling everyone about the kitten he keeps in a box. How he's going to slice it up and put the chunks in our soup."

Aunt Janet says, "Isn't he the one who made you go to the end of the line?"

Mary nods.

"Of all the guards to mess with," Aunt Janet says, "you had to pick him."

Mary says, "So now I don't know what to do."

Aunt Janet says, "Have you told anyone else?"

Mary says, "Just you."

Aunt Janet says, "Not even your husband?"

Mary says, "I haven't gone up to see him because I don't want Mr. Hendricks to take it out on him if they figure out it's me."

Aunt Janet says that could happen. Then she asks about the baby.

Mary says, "I think James has an ear infection. I ground up a little of the aspirin and mixed it in some water. That seems to take the edge off the fever but only for a while. What he really needs are antibiotics. He almost died from an ear infection six months ago."

Aunt Janet says, "Did you ask Mr. Hendricks for the medication?"

Mary says, "I waited in that awful line for almost a whole day. I could feel James burning up in my arms and that guard wouldn't even listen. When I did finally see Mr. Hendricks, he wouldn't listen either. He said sick babies aren't a priority. He told me to trade my rations with someone for the meds, then sent me out the door. Eight hours in line for thirty seconds, maybe."

Aunt Janet says, "Mr. Hendricks took control of a dangerous situation. Securing the food needed to be done. But separating the men and women, and the way he uses that evil guard, Mr. Smith—I think he's crossed a line and can't come back."

Mary says, "So what do I do?"

Two women walk by on the way to the buckets. Aunt Janet says something in a louder voice about how lousy the soup was. As soon as the women are gone, she's back to whispering. "Do you still have the vodka?"

Mary says, "Yes."

Aunt Janet says, "Okay. Tomorrow morning I want you to tell the big guard with the ponytail—he's the nicest of the bunch—that you know who the thief is and you want to see Mr. Hendricks right away."

Mary starts to argue, but Aunt Janet cuts her off.

"Tell Mr. Hendricks that you smelled alcohol on my breath and saw me sneaking some pills out of a bottle."

Mary begins to cry. She's trying to talk but can't. Aunt Janet tells her to take a deep breath, she'll be okay, she can do this. It takes a few moments, but Mary pulls herself together.

She says, "What will you do?"

Aunt Janet says, "I'll figure something out. Who knows, maybe I'm like that cat in the box. Maybe I have nine lives, too. Now, quick, while no one's looking—give me that bottle of vodka and a couple of aspirin."

- PRAY FOR ME -

I'm in my room having a "conversation" with Dutch, asking him what I should do about Lynn, who I was going out with in the pre-POD world, and this new girl, Amanda, who lives in the apartments across the street and has blown me kisses but is playing hard to get. Dutch says, Dude, what's your problem? I say, Should I feel guilty because Amanda is pushing Lynn out of my brain? Dutch says, It's not like you're marrying her or anything, it's just a couple of harmless blow kisses. It's all good, Dude, so go for it. I would.

It's amazing how much Dutch sounds like Alex.

I know this is certifiably nuts, asking a habitual ball-licker for relationship advice, but it's no crazier than the other actor in our little drama. Now I'm noticing every little thing he does, like if there's a piece of blue lint on the rug in the living room, two hours later it's gone. Or the spiderwebs in the skylight, which were there one day and gone the next. I never see him doing these things, so that means he's at it when I'm not looking or when I'm sleeping. Staying up late to scrub those counters is taking its toll. He's lost ten pounds at least and is ragged around the eyes. If he's shooting for a prisoner-of-war look, mission freaking accomplished.

Another thing that's driving me crazy is how I have these habits that won't die. Like opening the refrigerator and standing there as if a tuna salad sandwich will miraculously appear. When I walk into my room at night my hand searches for the light switch, and I still look for the clock on the microwave. But the absolute worst is my iPod— the craving to use that has got to be stronger than a cocaine habit.

This is the mental minefield I'm waltzing through when I smell it.

Smoke.

Something is definitely burning. I run down the stairs. It's stronger down here. Where's it coming from? Dad is looking out the living room window. His face has a strange orange glow.

He turns to me and says, "It's bad, Josh."

I run to the window and look across the street. A black, swirling plume is rising from the apartments. It is so thick you can hardly see the POD spinning above it. Angry orange flames shoot through windows on the second floor, and sections of the roof have that same sickening orange glow. A window smashes open on the fourth floor. The dancing woman pokes her head out in a billow of smoke and starts to scream. I pick up the binoculars, my heart pounding, and search for Amanda through the oily black. All I get is a single sheet of paper taped on the glass with these words:

pray 4 me josh. XO

I drop the binoculars. Bile rises sour in my throat. A door on the ground floor opens and two people run out. A man, then a woman carrying an infant. They're deleted before they reach the sidewalk. The dancing woman jumps from her window and disappears before hitting the ground.

"We shouldn't watch this," Dad says, his voice choked and raspy. He puts a hand on my shoulder. I shake it off.

"We have to do something," I say.

"There's nothing we can do."

"I can't just stand here," I say, moving toward the door. "Not again."

Dad lunges between me and the front door. "We have no choice, Josh."

The flames, raging tongues of orange and black, are soaring thirty feet above the roof. I feel the heat and smell the acrid smoke. The screams are a twisting knife in my chest. "Get out of my way."

Dad looks at me, eyes steady behind those glasses, shakes his head.

"Get out of my way!" I yell, this time making sure he knows that I'm going out that door no matter what he says or does.

Dad backs up against the door. He drops into a crouch, hands out like the wrestler he used to be, only he's bald, fifty-something, with a soft belly and a bad shoulder. And a pacemaker that doesn't work. I'm taller than him, and much faster. I have a brown belt in karate. On another day I'd be laughing.

"It's too early for this decision," he says.

"What decision?"

"To live or die."

"What's the point?" I move toward him. He tenses. "We'll die anyway when the food runs out, so we might as well make it mean something."

"There's still too much to live for."

"Like what? Powdered milk?" I keep moving, slow and steady. Only a couple of steps now...

"The PODs could go away, they could be defeated, they could... they could—"

I grab his left wrist and yank down hard. His eyes bug out like he can't believe I'm doing this. He's off balance, spinning down and away from the door. I push him into the wall, which he hits with a soft grunt. I'm at the door, releasing the deadbolt, then rotating the lock on the knob. Desperate fingers dig into my shoulder. He's saying No, no, no—you can't do this—don't do it...

It's all empty words to me. He won't go away. He wraps both arms around my waist, locking his hands in some wrestler move. Like the time he kept me from running to Jamie. Only this time it won't work. I'm trying to turn the knob but can't because he's pulling me back so hard. My hand is slipping, but suddenly the knob turns. The door swings open. There's flames and black smoke across the street, now double in size, while we fall backwards in a heap.

I push against him for leverage to stand up. He's surprisingly soft and nonresistant. Two seconds and I'm in the open doorway. I feel the heat. The smoke has a burnt hair smell that makes my stomach turn. I'm so ready for all this to be over.

There's a rasping, gurgling sound behind me. I turn to say good-bye.

Dad's on the floor, struggling to get up, eyes stunned, like a deer on the hunting channel that just fell over and can't see the arrow in its ribs. He's reaching out with one hand and clawing at his chest with the other. The color is draining from his face.

Without thinking, I know what to do. Mom and I have been through this drill with Dad—twice. I kneel beside him. Check his breathing. Shallow but there. Okay. Take his pulse. It's thin, irregular. At least he doesn't need CPR—yet. I have this crazy urge to open my cell phone and call 911.

"Dad," I say, my voice loud and firm, "can you hear me?"

His eyes slide open. They're jittery, like he can't figure out where to focus.

"Dad, where are your pills?"

He doesn't respond.

"Dad! Your pills! Where are they?"

He whispers, "Next to the sink in...in my bathroom."

I take off my sweatshirt and put it under his head. I sprint upstairs three at a time, slam into his bathroom, find the brown bottle with the big red heart on the front.

When I get back, he's still lying on the floor. I take his pulse. It's thready but there.

Behind him, through the open doorway, the flames rage on. But the screaming, mercifully, has stopped.

I close the door, kneel beside him. "How many?" I ask, opening the bottle.

"Two."

I shake out two pills, put them in his hand. "Do you need water?"

"No."

He swallows the pills. I watch him take a deep breath, close his eyes. A minute passes. The color is returning to his face. He starts to sit up. I help him lean back against the wall.

"How're you feeling?"

He smiles weakly. "Like that guy in the movie *Alien*, when the chest-burster—"

"Can we not talk about aliens right now?" I ask, returning the smile.

"Good point."

"Should I take your pulse again?"

He nods. I reach out for his hand.

An explosion blows out the glass in our living room window. The door flies open, revealing a boiling ball of orange and black. The entire apartment building is beginning to collapse, the roof is caving in. Flaming debris landed on the edge of the cul-de-sac. Another thirty feet and it's on our roof. A wave of nausea sweeps over me. Alex lives next to the apartment building. I can't see his house, but I'm pretty sure I see another billow of smoke.

I kneel beside Dad. His eyes are open wide, and he's shaking his head.

"Don't worry," I say, the chaos of noise and heat behind me. "It's all over now. I'm...I'm okay."

I stand up to close the door. Then I see something on the living room carpet, buried in glass. I brush it off, pick it up, and carry it to the door. I think of Amanda and her sign. *Pray 4 me Josh.* I think of all those people with nowhere to go. I think of Jamie running toward me. The bicycle and newspapers still out there. A constant reminder of something I couldn't do—didn't do.

I throw the binoculars into the smoldering void. They land near the end of the driveway, skitter, and stop.

I think of the POD commander, up there, enjoying the barbecue.

"Go to hell," I whisper.

I close the door.

- POODLES AND DUCT TAPE -

I can't crawl another inch. My last glow stick is fading and spiderwebs coat my hair like a helmet. My elbows have blisters and I need to pee. If I stay in this wormhole sixty seconds longer I'm going to scream until my head explodes. There's a soft yellow light coming from a tunnel off to the left. That's where I'm going, no matter what.

As I crawl closer to the light there are voices. Two men. One is laughing. I'm at the corner, making the turn. The vent cover is straight ahead, maybe four feet away. Something smells warm and meaty, like a soup. Is this the kitchen? Did I finally get lucky? That would mean Cassie is close by.

One of the voices says, "Move. You're blocking my light."

I'm pretty sure that's the big kahuna himself, Mr. Hendricks.

The other voice says, "What you need is some special seasoning."

My good luck just turned bad. That's Richie.

"How 'bout some of this?" Richie says.

A loud, desperate mew fills my head.

I sprint-crawl the last few feet to the vent cover. It's all I can do not to smash it open. The mewing goes on and on. It's coming from somewhere to my left. Whatever he's doing to Cassie, she hates it.

"Put that creature away," Mr. Hendricks says. "You're getting fur in my stew."

"Aw, I think she likes the steam."

"As much as I hate cats, I never did acquire a taste for torturing them."

The agonizing sound stops.

Richie says, "Back in the box you go." Then, after a moment, "So what do you call this *con*-coction?"

Mr. Hendricks says, "Poodle Noodle Soup with Vodka Reduction and Spring Vegetables."

"That was a poodle Manny caught?"

"Yes, plus some other breed mixed in."

"I hope it's Chihuahua. I miss Mexican food."

I press my face to the vent and look around. The opposite wall has a rack of shelves with pots and pans and mixing bowls. There's a big metal sink, and next to that is a stack of boxes. Farther down to the right there's a double door. I think it's the kind that swings both ways. On my side of the room it's hard to see much. The vent must be next to a desk or table because something is in the way. But that could be a good thing. It means if I'm careful maybe I can crawl out of here without them seeing me.

Mr. Hendricks says, "What's the status of your elusive pirate?"

Richie says, "Haven't heard from him yet."

"Yet? It's been three days."

"He'll show up."

"I think you're overestimating his affection for this animal."

"He loves the cat. Wrote all about it in his journal. Named her Missie, Callie, something like that."

"Then you're underestimating his intelligence."

"Nah, he's not smart, just lucky is all."

There's a slurping sound. Mr. Hendricks says, "Hm—hand me the salt." After a moment, "There's this gaping hole in your plan, see. I could drive a truck through it. If I were in his position, I'd love the gun more than the pet."

I push just a little against the corners of the vent. Both screws on top are tight.

Richie says, "Maybe he's outta ammo. He fired at me 'n Ax, musta been what? Eight, ten rounds at least. Shot out some windows is all."

"Lucky you."

"Damn straight."

"Why didn't you mention this before?"

"Musta slipped my mind."

"Strange we didn't hear any shots."

"Strange things happen. That's a fact."

I push on the lower left corner. It's a little loose, and the lower right corner—no screw at all.

Mr. Hendricks says, "We can't risk one of the guests acquiring a gun, see. Not even if it's empty. You ever see the movie *Die Hard?*"

"Best Christmas movie ever."

"You remember what happened when Bruce Willis got the gun?"

"The elevator door opens and there's a dead guy with a sign on his shirt—"

"He started picking them off one at a time, you idiot! We don't want anyone going Die Hard on us."

The soup-slurping sound again.

"Either you bring me your so-called pirate or you bring me the weapon. Otherwise—someone has to be picked off first, and the obvious character is you."

I push a little harder on the lower left corner. The screw pops out with a clang, rolls on the hard tile to the middle of the floor, spins, and stops. I hold my breath.

Mr. Hendricks says, "You hear that?"

Richie says, "Probably our little friend. I'll check on her, make sure she's...*com*-fortable."

Mr. Hendricks says, "Hand me the oregano first. It's that green bottle next to the tomatoes."

The snakeskin boots move this way. Each clicking step feels like a kick in the head. He'll see the screw for sure. There's no time for me to back up far enough to get away. I chew on my lip and wait. The boots pass right in front of me, inches from the screw.

A door opens on my side of the wall. There's a muffled sound, like someone shouting into a pillow.

Richie says, "Is everything okay in here?"

More of that muffled sound. Who is that?

Richie says, "Aw, you can't breathe? You want me to re-move the tape?" He laughs. "Not in this lifetime, bitch."

The door closes. Boots clicking on tile. They stop at the screw.

He bends down, picks it up, looks around. For a second, the longest second of my life, he looks right at the vent. All I see from inside the hood is the shadowy outline of thin lips and one eye. It's small and dark and doesn't blink. He stands up, puts the screw in his pocket, moves on.

Back with Mr. Hendricks, Richie says, "So what's the plan for her?"

"We cannot tolerate theft. She steals, she suffers the consequences."

Mary? Aunt Janet?

"What are those *con*-sequences?"

"You can handle that after lunch. The poodle needs to simmer a little longer. First, let's check on the natives, make sure they're not getting restless."

Mr. Hendricks and Richie walk past the vent. The swinging doors open and close.

They're gone—for now.

I push on the bottom of the vent. It swings up like it's on hinges. I slide out and stand up. The rooms spins. It's been so long since I've been on my legs that they almost collapse. It takes a few seconds, a few seconds I don't have, for things to get right. I look around. A big stove. A steaming metal pot. Three burning candles on a counter. Some small tomatoes and a butcher knife. I run over to the tomatoes, cram them into my mouth. The juice explodes and dribbles down my chin. I could eat a hundred more.

Where's that box?

I see some up on a high shelf by the stove. Too high for me to reach. I shake the shelf. Pots and pans clang. But Cassie mews! She's up there. I search for something to step on. At the far end of the room—a chair!

Then I hear that muffled sound. Next to the vent there's a door with a window. It's an office or something. Someone is in there. My mind races. Cassie or the door? Cassie or the door? No time to think. I run to the door, look through the glass. It's dark, but I see a woman curled up on the floor. Her hands and feet are wrapped with duct tape. A strip of tape covers her mouth. She sees me looking in. Her eyes go buggy and she starts to struggle and moan.

I open the door, take the broken knife out of my pocket, kneel beside her. I slice through the tape around her wrists. She rips the tape off her mouth while I free her ankles.

She gasps, "Who are you?"

I know that voice. Aunt Janet. "I'm—I'm the Pirate."

Aunt Janet stands up. It's amazing—she's not much taller than me. And almost as thin. An idea is forming in my head. I scoop up the pieces of tape.

She whispers, "You're the Pirate? A girl? My God, you even have the eye patch."

I whisper back, "We need to go."

We slip out the door and close it behind us. I stop and listen. There are voices on the other side of the swinging doors. Someone coughs. Richie says, "Suck on a lozenge or something."

"Like where am I going to find that?"

"Then suck on your damn thumb. I don't care. I'm tired of you blowin' your germs in my face."

My eyes dart to the box on the shelf. Cassie is up there.

Richie says, "I'm thinking we haul her up to the roof, give the aliens some target practice."

Aunt Janet says, "What are you looking for?"

I point to the shelf and say, "Can you help me get that box?"

She looks at me like I'm insane.

Richie says, "Mmm. Smell that Poodle Noodle soup!"

He can't be more than seconds away. I leave the pieces of tape over by the door—it's part of my new escape plan—and whisper, "Follow me!" Dropping to my knees, I lift the vent cover and crawl back into the LTT.

She says, "You've got to be kidding."

But there's grunting behind me as she squeezes into the hole. I scoot forward, hit the T, and make the right turn. Her hands brush the bottoms of my feet.

We're scooting down the straightaway when a tornado slams into the kitchen. Pots and pans tossed around, glass breaking—it shakes the walls and is so loud it echoes in the wormhole.

Richie yells, "THE LONGER YOU HIDE, BITCH, THE MORE IT'S GONNA HURT!" Then a short scream, followed by "YOU ATE ALL THE TOMATOES!"

And somewhere, underneath all that noise, is a box with a small kitten inside. A helpless, scrawny kitten that purrs me to sleep when I'm scared and shivering in the dark. No time to think about that now. I pull the fading glow stick out of my pocket and clamp it between my teeth.

If I bite any harder I'll snap it in half.

We're at the vent above the utility room. I didn't make any wrong turns getting here, which is lucky and amazing since the glow stick is almost dead. Aunt Janet told me she was impressed with my sense of direction. I showed her the tape markings and she was even more impressed.

We stop and listen. The door is locked, plus there's tape jammed in the key slot, so chances are good no one is lurking inside. The ladder is still there. It's a little tricky because the room is dark and we come out head first, but Aunt Janet holds my feet while I climb on, and then I hold the ladder steady for her.

My escape plan was that Richie would find the pieces of duct tape by the swinging doors, which would give him the idea that Aunt Janet was hiding around the kitchen. It was pretty lame, but I think he fell for it. Hopefully that bought us enough time to sneak into the parking garage and make it to the cave. The only problem is I should have Cassie with me, and I don't.

Richie isn't waiting in the utility room. He's not on the other side of the access door. I have the pepper spray in my hand, just in case. We wait in the shadows of the stairwell, but the parking garage seems empty. It could be a trap, but I tell Aunt Janet to follow me. We stay low, run past the Nova and the SUV, around the corner, and up the ramp to Level 2. I crouch behind another car, look and listen. No Richie. This is feeling way too easy. What choice do I have? I tell Aunt Janet to wait here. I run to the Suburban, open the rear hatch, peel back the carpet, lift the trapdoor, wave for her to join me. She runs up, panting like a dog.

"Feet first, face up," I say. "It's easier to get out."

She climbs in. I take one last look around, close the rear hatch, slip into the cave, drop the lid, and test the seal. Good. The carpet is back in place.

There are tiny drips of light leaking in through the airholes. They look like stars in a midnight sky. There really isn't enough light to see anything, but looking at them makes me feel better. We're both breathing hard, which makes the air feel hot and heavy. It takes a few seconds to get settled. The cave is tall enough for us to lie on our sides, but only if we scrunch our shoulders. On our backs is definitely the best position. We're like sardines in a can. I can't get over how strange it feels to have another person around, someone who can actually talk. For the moment, though, neither one of us is talking.

After a minute or so, Aunt Janet whispers, "What's your real name?"

"Meghan," I whisper. "That's with an 'h.' But everyone calls me Megs."

"How old are you, Megs with an 'h'?"

"I'm twelve. But I'll be thirteen on July fourth."

"You were born on Independence Day? That doesn't surprise me."

"Mom said I was her little firecracker."

"Where are your parents?"

It takes me a couple of seconds to work this one out. "My father...Mom thinks he's dead. She's probably right, because he was a drug addict. He left when I was little. My mom drove off with some guy on a job interview right before the spaceballs came. I know she's alive, I just don't know where."

"Where is home?"

"Erie, Pennsylvania."

"Your mom had a job interview at five in the morning?"

"We were out of money. She said it would be a short job and then we'd eat breakfast at Denny's and then go to the beach. I've never even seen the beach."

"You've been living alone out here all this time?"

I wasn't alone, but I don't feel like explaining it, so I say nothing.

Aunt Janet waits, then says, "What happened to your eye?"

"I bumped it while I was hiding under a car four days ago."

"Where did you get the bandage?"

"I found a first-aid kit. It's right here behind me."

"When did you last change it?"

"I haven't. It really hurts."

"I need to look at it." She starts sliding toward the trapdoor. "There's lots of swelling around—"

I grab her arm. "Don't!" I whisper. The truth is, I'm afraid it will hurt too much just taking off the bandage. So I say, "It's not safe yet. He's out there. I can feel it."

She stops, moves back next to me. She touches my arm and says, "You're an amazing young girl, Megs."

I say, "What's your name?"

All of a sudden I shiver, like I'm cold from the inside out. But it doesn't make sense since I'm sweating.

"Carrie. That's with a 'C.'"

"Can I call you Aunt Janet?"

She laughs. "Okay—if I can call you Pirate."

It's quiet again. I like it better when we're whispering. That way I don't think about how much my head hurts. I'm really feeling cold now. My teeth are starting to chatter.

Aunt Janet says, "Back there in the kitchen – what was in the box?"

I don't want to say anything. But I can't help myself. My throat tightens, like I'm going to choke. "Cassie, my kitten."

Aunt Janet says, "Oh, no. My God—that was your cat? Oh, Megs. I'm so sorry."

I'm crying now. It hurts, but I can't stop. She reaches out, pulls me into her arms. She doesn't smell that good, but I don't care.

She says, "You saved my life, Pirate. Thank you."

I choke out, "You're welcome." I can hardly talk I'm shivering so hard. But in the back of my head I'm already thinking. Thinking about tomorrow and the wormhole and the box.

Aunt Janet says, "My God, girl, you're burning up!"

Then, in a swirling, falling instant, I'm not thinking at all.

- DOWN THE DRAIN -

I catch Dutch in the bathroom, drinking out of the tub. But I'm too late. He must have bumped the drain lever with his head, because the tub is nearly empty. All our water, our survival, down the drain. It's my job to keep him out of the bathroom and I didn't and now I'm afraid to tell Dad, but he's going to find out anyway. I take Dutch and put him in my room. Then I return the drain to the plugged position and call Dad.

"It was like this when I found it," I say.

He's staring at something. I follow his eyes. There's fresh drool and water stains on the rug.

"Must be a leak," I say.

"Must be," he says quietly. He walks out the door.

"Maybe it'll rain," I say to his back.

"Maybe," he says from the hall.

Dutch hears us and starts to bark.

Looking at the trail of drool on the carpet, Dad says, "You can let him out now, Josh. What's done is done." He slips into his bedroom and shuts the door.

DAY 21: LOS ANGELES, CALIFORNIA

- BREAKING MIRRORS -

"Shh. Megs, you have to be quiet. Do you understand?"

A voice in the dark whispers to me. It's a woman's voice. Why is she whispering? Where am I?

The voice says, "Richie is out there. I think someone is with him."

My clothes are soaked. A blanket is over me, and it's wet. My skin burns like glowing coals. But I'm shivering, shivering so hard my bones ache.

There are other voices beyond the dark. They are yelling. Broken words leak into this place, but I can't understand them. A warm hand strokes my hair and pulls me close.

The woman's voice says, "They'll leave soon. Then we can get you out of these wet clothes."

I want to say that my throat hurts, but the words get stuck.

She must know my thoughts because something cool and wet is pressed to my cracked lips. Two small sips and she takes it away.

The voices outside are close. They mix with a sound like thunder. It hurts my ears. Something is shaking this dark place. Is it the wind...?

I give in to the blackness swirling inside my head. It turns into a gray fog that forms into a man. I recognize this man. I'm looking at his reflection in a big mirror. The mirror cracks, then shatters. I turn around. He's standing in front of me holding something over a steaming pot on a stove. It's a baby. The baby is crying.

This man—I know his eyes. At first I think it's Richie. Then he laughs and begins counting down.

5...4...3...2...1...

The man is Mr. Hendricks.

I try to scream but can't because a hand clamps down on my mouth. I pull and scratch at the fingers, but they're too strong and firm and won't let go.

"It's okay," the voice whispers. "Shhh. Shhh. They're almost gone, honey. It will be okay. Shhh..."

The outside voices fade, the wind stops, the thunder rolls away. The hand slides off my mouth.

Someone is stroking my hair. My mother strokes my hair.

I give in to the gentle tug of sleep.

Dad and I aren't speaking to each other. Which, given our situation, means we're not speaking at all. This isn't because we're mad or anything. I think it's because, after all this imprisonment and impending doom, we've finally run out of things to talk about. The bathtub incident may have triggered this explosion of silence, but I saw Dad scratching Dutch's ears today, so how mad can he be?

But here's how crazy things are:

Dad shows up in my room an hour ago with the Scrabble game. He shakes the box and points downstairs, like *Do you want to play?* I shrug, like *Why the hell not*, and follow him down to the table.

We pick our chips, decide who goes first, and start to play, all in complete and total silence. He doesn't whine about his letters; he doesn't call me a cheater when my third word, TURDIEST, scores eighty-seven points. It's the weirdest freaking thing ever. Weirder than the rows and columns in the pantry and even his obsession with keeping the counters spotless and germ free.

So I'm killing him by at least a hundred points when my arm starts tingling. He puts down LISP to score twelve. I wait for the blackness, then the flash. I smile and put down my word, QUIVERS, for so many points I have trouble adding them in my head. I'm thinking this will do it—he's going to crack and say something—when someone yells "Help!" outside our window. That has to be Mr. Conrad.

We run to the living room. There's a plastic sheet covering the hole where the big picture window used to be. I don't spend much time in here anymore. The view sucks.

Dad is cranking open the window on the side facing Mr. Conrad's house.

I'm looking out the front door.

He's calling to Mr. Conrad, asking him what's wrong.

I'm wondering where the hell the POD went.

Mr. Conrad yells, "Elaine—she's in trouble."

Dad yells, "What kind of trouble?"

I want to tell him that something is up with the PODs, but he's too involved in his conversation. For a second I think about walking outside. That would get his attention.

Mr. Conrad yells back, "She has a terrible headache. It's so bad she threw up. Can you spare some ibuprofen? We're completely out."

I locate the POD, off to the left and up a lot higher.

Dad says, "How will we get it to you?"

While they work that out—Mr. Conrad says something about giving us crackers in exchange—I run to the patio door for a view of the backyard PODs. They're there, all the way to the horizon, but definitely not as many. And the ones that are left are moving to higher positions. It's amazing to watch, these huge black balls floating upward silent and slow, like bubbles rising in shampoo. Some disappear in the clouds; most stay just below them. This process must have started while we were playing Scrabble. If it weren't for Mr. Conrad, I would have missed the big event. The POD commander keeps 'em flashing, though, just in case the inmates have crazy thoughts about leaving the prison.

Dad is calling me back to the living room. The game of who can go the longest without talking to the other person is officially over—and I'm the champ. Mr. Conrad is looking at us through his open bedroom window. His gray hair, thin and wispy like smoke, hangs in loose strands over his face, which is startlingly cadaverlike. He's wearing a blue denim shirt with dark stains and missing buttons. Definitely not the robust, meticulously dressed, ready-for-church-on-Sunday look I'm used to. He offers a feeble wave and I wave back.

Dad pulls me away from the window and whispers, "He wants us to send Dutch over with some pills."

It seems like a reasonable idea. Dutch likes the Conrads and they like him. They take care of him when we go out of town, and

Mr. and Mrs. Conrad take him for walks in the summer, or used to, before they got sick and Dutch's hip went bad.

I say, "Great. Let's do it."

I call for Dutch. He limps in from the kitchen and sits down.

"How about it, Dutch?" I say. His tail thumps the floor at the sound of his name. "You want to be a hero?"

Dutch licks his nose, his dog brain sensing a walk and the possibility of a treat.

Dad says, "This doesn't concern you?"

"Should it?"

"What if they keep him?"

"For a pet?"

"For a meal."

"The Conrads? You're kidding, right?"

He says nothing. But his eyes say it all.

I remember the apartment fire, Jamie behind the car, my feeling of helplessness. I don't want Mrs. Conrad dying because I'm too selfish to lend the services of our dog.

"This is our chance to help someone," I say. "They won't keep Dutch."

"What if they do?"

"They won't."

I return his stare. After a long second Dad says, "Fine. He's your dog."

Dad counts out twenty ibuprofens and puts them in a baggie. I duct-tape the baggie to Dutch's front left leg. We tie a rope, a hundred feet long, to his collar, to keep him from wandering off. The POD commander is spinning in his new location, no doubt keeping an eye on things. My eyes drift to the bike and I think: *It would be so easy just to walk out the door. End it all in a flash of light.* But I want to see how this little drama plays out. Be the hero. Save Mrs. Conrad.

I open the door and send Dutch outside. Mr. Conrad calls to him. He trots over, tail wagging in anticipation of a treat, just like in the old, pre-POD days. Their front door opens. He walks into their house.

After about thirty seconds Dad says, "This isn't right. Pull the rope."

"Just relax," I say. "He's giving him a treat."

"Josh, just pull the rope."

"Why are you always so paranoid when all—"

Dutch starts to walk outside. A hand grabs his collar and yanks him back. He yelps.

I stand there, frozen, not sure what to do or think.

Dad screams, "Pull the *freaking* rope!"

I react, but it's too late. The door slams shut. I pull twice on the rope and it finally jerks free. We reel it in and examine the end. There are no frayed or ragged threads. It is sliced cleanly at an angle.

Dad says, "I knew it. I knew this was going to happen."

At that instant I have this bizarre thought: *Now he's talking to me and I wish he weren't.*

My heart is pounding. The living room spins. I feel dizzy and angry and I can't breathe. I lunge for the door but Dad holds me from behind. I don't care anymore. All I want is for this to be over. I long for the light, for that microsecond of instant release.

I jerk my head backwards. It connects with a dull thud. Then I'm lifted off the floor and on my back, Dad's on top of me saying it's all right, it wasn't my fault. Blood is gushing from his nose. I can't hear him because my arms are swinging and my brain is screaming for a freedom I can't have.

Like a blanket over a fire, the room goes black.

- VOICES IN THE DARK –

Richie found me. He's breaking into the cave. I try to slide away from the opening, but it's hard to move. Everything is so heavy, even the blanket. I can hardly lift my arms. A beam of light shoots down, burning my eyes. A blurry hand appears. It's holding something. A knife?

I scream.

The voice whispers, "Shhh!"

I scream again.

"Megs, it's me! It's okay."

Another arm, a shoulder...

I drag myself backwards. My shoulder bumps against something hard. I can't go any farther. I pull the blanket over my head, close my eyes, and curl into a shivering ball.

He's moving toward me. There's nowhere to hide.

He peels the blanket away. His hand touches my forehead.

The voice says, "You're still too hot." Then, "God, I wish I had a thermometer." Then, "I couldn't read it anyway."

I'm starting to understand.

Not Richie. Someone else. Someone else—Aunt Janet.

I say between shivers, "I thought...I thought you were him. You had a knife."

She says, "I'm sorry I scared you."

"Where did you go?"

"To find more water. You're sweating so much. You need fluids to fight this infection."

"I'm sorry I screamed."

"No more talking, Pirate. You need to rest. Here, open your mouth. Take this pill." She puts something small in my mouth. "Now drink this."

She puts a bottle to my lips. I drink. It's water. "Where did you—"

"Shhh. We can talk later. Right now you need to sleep."
She wraps me in the blanket, puts her arms around me.
My shivering slows, then stops.
I close my eyes.

DAY 23: PROSSER, WASHINGTON

- BACK TO NORMAL -

My eye is swollen shut where Dad hauled off and slugged me. But that's okay. I think I broke his nose when I gave him the headbutt. It looks like a bruised banana. And his right eye is so puffed up his glasses don't fit right. He says the swelling would go down faster if we had ice or even a wet rag to put on it. But those items are ancient history, artifacts from some long-dead civilization. After the bathtub incident we are now in severe water-rationing mode. We need what's left of the water, the little we could drain from the hot-water tank, for drinking. I swallow the remaining ibuprofen dry. After this I'll just have to deal with the headaches. Dad says my eye will be back to normal in a week or two.

A week or two—now there's a thought. What will life be like? Hmm...actually it's not that hard to predict. It's like I'm reading a book with exactly the same words in every chapter. Turn the page, same damn thing. Might as well skip to the end and get it over with.

And normal—there's an interesting word. I look around the house. Most of the furniture is in pieces, but after the apartments burned down Dad was afraid to use the fireplace. So the pieces sit in a useless pile. We're using cut-up sheets for toilet paper. When that's gone we'll use the towels. Dad has already cut some of them into perfect four-inch squares. The refrigerator door hangs open, a silent reminder of how screwed up things really are. The pantry—I wouldn't even call what's left a snack. Outside our house the garbage is piling up. We toss all the empty cans out the back door, and the side yard has a respectable mound of toilet paper, cut-up sheets, and, to quote Dad, defecation.

At night we burn candles, but eventually they'll be gone too. When that happens, we will be swallowed up by the darkness that has consumed our neighborhood, our towns, our cities, our planet.

And the PODs hang over it all. Sometimes they're all I can see.
Sometimes I forget they're there.

The good news is that I can walk by a light switch without feeling the urge to turn it on.

And the bad news?

At night, when I should be sleeping, I still hear Dutch licking his balls.

- SAVED BY THE PILL -

It's light outside, but just barely. I'm naked in the back seat of the Suburban, the horse blanket wrapped tight around me. I have no idea how many days I've been sleeping. One, two, five? For once, my brain clock is confused. Aunt Janet watches me from the front seat. The windshield behind her is a huge spiderweb of broken glass.

I don't like being out of the cave like this.

"Good morning, Pirate," she says.

"Good morning." I rub my eyes, then stop. There's a fresh bandage with fresh, hair-pulling tape.

"You can probably take that off," she says.

I peel away the bandage, grateful to have both eyes open. "Why don't I have my clothes on?"

"You soaked them twice, killing that fever. I could have boiled water on your forehead."

"Why are we out here?"

"It's too hot in the hideout. I had to risk it."

"Shouldn't we get back in the cave?"

"In a bit. The inside needs to air out a little more." She reads my look. "The Evil One has had some busy nights. He needs his beauty sleep."

The Evil One. I like that. "How long was I sick?"

"Three days. I thought I'd lost you—until I found this." She holds up the azith pill bottle. "Where did you get it?"

"The sleeping pills? I found those when I was scrounging for food."

Something moves off to my left. I find it. A seagull sits on the concrete barrier, then flies away.

"They're not sleeping pills," she says. "It's azithromycin, a prescription antibiotic."

"I almost took them one night when I couldn't sleep."

"You're very lucky you had them. They saved your life."

Staying out like this is getting on my nerves. Even the seagulls are freaking me out. Sunlight is shrinking the shadows. I sit up.

"Can I have my clothes?"

Aunt Janet reaches down, picks up my things, and tosses them to me, saying, "They're probably dry by now."

She turns her back while I dress. They're still a little damp, but close enough. And the smell—I'm used to that.

With my clothes on I feel better. Like I can run if I need to.

I say, "Are you a nurse?"

Aunt Janet laughs. "I'm a school librarian. But I'm a mother, and all mothers are part-time nurses." She studies my face and says, "Megs, what do you remember?"

"I remember you said something about Richie and that I needed to be quiet. I remember being sure he was in the cave, that he had a knife. I remember being hot and cold at the same time. That's about it. Oh, and the car was shaking. I thought it was from the thunder."

She smiles. "We had a storm all right. Hurricane Richie."

I think about that for a moment, then say, "I did have a dream, though."

I tell her about the baby over the steaming pot and the countdown. About Richie turning into Mr. Hendricks. She takes it all in without saying anything. Her eyes—a soft brown with flecks of green—are hard to read. When I'm done, she's quiet, then opens her mouth to say something, stops, and looks away. Like she's trying to figure out what to put out there, the truth or something else.

She says, "You found a great hiding spot, Megs. The Evil One and his pal hit every car, including this one, on the first three levels."

"How do you know?"

"I had to look for water."

I remember her giving me something to drink.

"Where did you find the water?"

"The fluid reservoirs for the windshield washers. Sometimes people just put in water."

"You said he was yelling?"

"Screaming is more like it," she says. "I believe he's possessed by demons."

"What was he saying?"

There's that look again. Like she's measuring one choice against another. I used to get the same thing from Mom after her fights with Zack. I'd ask about the red spots and the bruises. She'd give me that same look and try to hide things by changing the subject and lighting cigarettes, one after the other. After Zack moved in she lit a lot of cigarettes.

I'm pretty sure I know what Aunt Janet isn't saying.

"Richie said something about Cassie, right?"

"Yes, and some other things too. Bad things. But now isn't the time to talk about it."

"Why? Why can't you tell me now?"

"Because you were—you *are*—a very sick girl. The infection almost killed you and—"

"But I'm better now." I sit up straight and tall. "Tell me what he said."

"You won't go crazy on me?"

"I promise."

Aunt Janet leans forward and says, "Richie must have figured out that I'm in the garage with you. He said Mr. Hendricks has a message for us. If we turn in the gun, he'll give the baby the medicine. Otherwise"—she turns away at this, her voice cracking—"he said the aliens will get some baby food."

"Did he say anything about Cassie?"

"Yes."

I wait. Silence booms in the front seat.

"What did he say?"

Aunt Janet turns to me and says, "That she tasted like chicken."

All those thoughts I had about Richie come boiling to the top. I reach for the door handle, ready to jump out. Aunt Janet is saying something about plans for tomorrow. I'm not listening. My brain is locked on the wormhole, the gun, and pointing the barrel at

Richie's smiling, evil face. But none of that happens. As soon as I open the door, my head spins like a Tilt-A-Whirl. I see all these crazy colors and almost fall to the pavement. I slide back into the car and close my eyes. Everything is still spinning.

Aunt Janet says, "Do you really have the gun?"

"I think so. It's in a briefcase that's locked, so I don't know for sure. I hid it."

"Where?"

"I wedged it under the seat in my mom's car on the first level."

"What are you planning to do with it?" she asks.

"I'm going to shoot Richie in the head."

"You can't do that. It's not—"

"Yes I can, so shut up!"

"Don't talk to me like that, please."

"He's a monster. He doesn't deserve to live."

"Have you ever shot someone, Megs?"

The only gun I've ever had in my hand squirted water. But I'm not about to tell her.

She looks at me hard. "I asked you if you've ever shot someone?"

"No," I say. "Not yet."

"I didn't think so," she says. "Me either, and I don't think I could."

"Well, I know I can," I say.

"And how does a twelve-year-old girl know this?"

I think about it, then say, "Because I'm a pirate, and that's what pirates do."

- THE BROOD -

And yet again, the screeching.

Only this time it's different. I had an episode just before it happened. Up to this point I thought the flash of light was the main event. Now I'm not so sure. There's more to the moment of blackness that comes right before it. Like I should pay more attention, maybe stretch it out. I'm not sure how or why, but that's what I'm chewing on when my head fills with the freaking alien noise.

Once the nausea passes and my brain clears, I head downstairs. Dad is standing in front of the dining room window. The shade is up. He's in sweatpants and a pajama top, looking out at the PODs. I'm amazed at how thin he is. But his beard is trimmed and his hair is combed. Part hippie, part engineer. I wonder if Mom would recognize him. The broken nose doesn't help.

He says, "They've stopped spinning."

I stand beside him at the window. Large blood-red circles are forming on the bottom of the PODs. The circles spread outward and up, almost to a point where the bottom halves become entirely red. I have to remind myself to breathe.

A massive hole opens in the bottom of the PODs.

Then, like swarms of bees from mother hives, small black dots pour out of the holes. They form pulsing black clouds, shimmering like hot oil as they literally fill the sky. Patches of blue sky become smaller and smaller, then disappear as the swarms merge. Their shadows cover the ground. An early-evening darkness falls upon us, even though it's still morning. We watch in stunned silence. The PODs continue to bleed out, and it feels like it will never end. Whatever they plan on doing, I hope it's quick and I hope it doesn't hurt.

There's a humming sound, slowly getting louder. The window-pane shakes. Even glasses in the cabinet over the sink are vibrating.

Dad says, "Do you think Mom is watching this?"

"You think she's alive?" I ask.

"Yes, I do. I dream about her almost every night."

"I thought you didn't dream."

"I do now."

The mini-PODs have formed into funnels that spiral to the ground.

I want to ask if that's a good thing, Mom being alive to see this. I want to say, *Why didn't you let me walk out the door? Why did you let me send Dutch? Why do I have to die with my eye swollen shut?* But instead I say, "I dream about her, too."

Dad turns away from the window. I think his shoulders are shaking, but I'm not sure. I've never seen him cry, although I've heard a strange moaning sound coming from his room. He rubs his beard, draws a breath, and says, "Let's have that last chocolate bar for breakfast. For some reason I feel like celebrating."

We sit down for what could be our last meal. He carefully breaks the bar in two, putting each portion on a separate plate. Why we can't just eat it out of our hand is a mystery to me. My slab is the biggest, of course. We accompany the feast with a half glass of warm, murky water from the bottom of the hot-water tank. I taste each individual flake of rust.

But the chocolate, I must admit, is the best ever.

I've always wondered what is inside the PODs, and now I know. Mini-PODs. The black dots are really smaller versions of the mother ships, with one notable difference. There is a single black stalk sticking up from the very top like a middle finger. Otherwise the surface is smooth and glistens as though it's covered with a thin layer of oil. I know this because I see them outside the dining room window. In fact, if there wasn't the minor issue of being deleted, I could open the window and touch one of the brood with my hand. At first they made a low-level buzz. Now they do their thing in silence.

That thing is to hover a couple of feet above the ground and move in what at first seemed to be random circles and lines. After a while it became clear that there was nothing random about them. The mini-PODs organized into huge brood-squares easily the size of three or four football fields. They move in slow, meticulous, grid-like patterns. Even though they cover the earth like robotic beetles and often pass within inches of each other, they never touch. And while this is going on, squirrels scamper across the grass, robins fly around building nests, and massive flocks of geese, free from hunters, fill the sky. It's just your average spring day on the planet.

There is another observation worth bringing up: the mini-PODs avoid the houses. After that heart-pounding instant when they left the sky and descended to earth, it's been pretty boring. We waited for them to spray poison gas or morph into killer robots, but nothing dramatic happened. After an hour, things settled into this meticulous, ground-hugging infestation.

Meanwhile, the mother PODs are rotating.

Dad is sitting at the kitchen table, drawing graphs in his notebook.

I guess breakfast is canceled.

DAY 25: LOS ANGELES, CALIFORNIA

- CRACKING THE OYSTER -

It's a sunny morning, but that doesn't matter. Like we're going to the beach or something—ha! Instead of a bathing suit, I'm wearing camo pants, and instead of suntan lotion and candy, my pockets bulge with other treasures, like pepper spray, a knife, a cigarette lighter, tape, and a screwdriver.

No, today will definitely not be a day at the beach.

We sneak down to the Nova, ducking behind cars and watching for you-know-who. Twice I have to wait for Aunt Janet while she bends over like someone punched her in the stomach. She said it's nothing to worry about, just a little gas cramp from the jerky we had for breakfast. I don't know about that. I heard her groaning in the dark last night. If it really is gas, then we need to find her something else to eat.

After the second "cramp" I start to seriously worry about Aunt Janet's plan, which she explained to me this morning while we waited for the sun to come up. It basically goes like this:

We slip into the hotel through the LTT.

We wait in the kitchen for Mr. Hendricks, or even better, Mr. Hendricks and Richie.

Aunt Janet threatens to shoot them while I tape up their hands and feet.

She guards them while I find Mary and Lewis, her sick baby.

I give Mary six azith pills—that leaves us with ten.

We exit like bandits through the LTT.

We jump into the hideout, close the hatch, and wait out the storm.

Oh, I forgot—we take some water and food from the hotel before we go.

I'm thinking Aunt Janet has seen too many movies. There's all kinds of craziness in this plan. Like, what if they shoot us with their guns first? Or what if I can't find Mary? Or they take me hostage and threaten to shoot *me?* Obviously she's not good at making these kinds of plans. But I don't rain on her parade—yet. I figure we get the gun, then I'll tell her about my plan.

The Nova is exactly the same. There's still pieces of red plastic under the taillights from when Richie smashed them with the hammer. Aunt Janet keeps an eye on the green door while I dig out the briefcase from under the seat and set it on the pavement.

We start out trying to pry it open with the screwdriver. That is such a waste of time. I get a lug wrench from the SUV. She wedges in the screwdriver while I pry with the lug wrench. It looks like the case is about to pop when Black Beard opens the green door. I ease pressure off the lug wrench and the case snaps shut. Black Beard looks around, drops his pants, squats over the bucket, and whistles. We hide behind the car and wait. I close my eyes. I mean, like, who wants to watch that? After a few minutes we hear the green door open and close. Instantly we're back to work on the briefcase. Thirty-two minutes, five seconds, and one bloody knuckle later, the case splits open like an oyster.

The pearl is a big black handgun snuggled in a nest of gray foam. Aunt Janet picks up the gun, turns it over in her hands.

She says, "Glock .31 357 SIG." Her hands move. There's a metallic snapping sound. In one smooth motion almost too fast to see, the thing that holds the bullets drops out of the handle, she catches it with her left hand, looks at it, frowns, slams it back in. "Fifteen-round clip, empty."

My eyes are as wide as Frisbees. "How did you...?"

She shrugs. "My father was a cop, okay? He collected guns. He used to take me to the shooting range every Sunday after church."

"So we don't have any bullets?"

"Not a single one. That means we have to—"

Her face twists. She drops the gun, grabs her head.

The screeching explodes between my ears.

We fall to the floor, twisting and moaning in the dirt and glass. It hurts me bad, but I think it's killing Aunt Janet. When it's finally over I know something is wrong. She can barely sit up. Her face is the color of oatmeal, and what little we had for breakfast is all over her shirt. There's a thin trail of bubbly pink stuff oozing down her chin. Her body is shaking.

She crawls over to the car, leans back against the door.

I say, "I hate it when they do that."

She opens her mouth to talk but can't get out the words. Her eyes are all twitchy and her breathing is short and fast, like something is squeezing her lungs.

"Are you okay?" It's a stupid question, because I can see she isn't. But I don't know what else to say.

Her head moves. I can't tell if it's a yes or a no.

There's a flash of yellow light—it lasts for five seconds—and then things get very dark, very fast. Then there's a soft hum, like I'm sitting under a tree full of bees.

I say, "I think the aliens are coming."

She motions for me to come close.

The buzzing isn't so soft anymore. I place my ear next to her lips.

She whispers, "Help me stand up."

I wrap her left arm around my shoulder. She struggles to her feet. I hold her steady while we walk to the nearest wall and look up at the sky. My legs almost crumble again. The spaceballs moved way up high—and they're having babies. Millions of them. Each spaceball has a huge hole in the bottom, and the babies are pouring out like black ink from a bottle. The sky is covered with big ugly stains spreading outward. When the stains come together they form into funnel-like tornados that spiral toward the ground. I count at least five tornados. I can't see what happens next because buildings are in the way. Truth is, I don't want to see.

Aunt Janet says, "So it's finally happening."

"What is?"

"What they came here to do."

Whatever that is, it can't be good. "We need to hide," I say, trying hard to keep my voice from shaking. I think the utility room is a good spot because it has two metal doors. Or even the Suburban. Anything is better than hanging out here like this. We might as well be standing under a *Here's Dinner* sign.

But instead of running, Aunt Janet says, "I wonder if they're watching?" Her voice is far-off, like she's someplace else. Her head drops and she takes these short, gaspy breaths. I think she's crying, that she's giving up. Then she looks up at the sky and screams: "LEAVE US ALONE!"

What she just did makes about as much sense as an ice cube yelling at the sun. It seems to help, though. There's some red in her cheeks and her eyes aren't empty anymore. In fact, they look the *opposite* of empty when she turns to me and says, "We're changing the plan."

That's a relief, is what I think. "Good," is what I say.

Behind her the first of the babies are floating down like basketball-sized snowflakes. They stop about two feet off the ground. They're black and shiny with a short pointer on top.

"You have to go into the hotel," she says. "Alone."

I say, "Why can't you come?"

Her eyes cloud. Her body tenses, then sags. She says between breaths, "I'm too sick. You'd...you'd be safer without me. I'm sorry."

My stomach is twisting like snakes in a sack. But I say, "That's all right. I've done it before."

I help Aunt Janet drag herself to the SUV. I'd rather hide her in the cave, but she'd never make it that far. She crawls into the back seat. I sprint back to the Suburban, snag the horse blanket. By the time I'm back she's asleep. I cover her with the blanket.

It's not dark anymore. The floaters—that's what I call them now—stopped falling from the sky. Now they're all over the street and sidewalks, moving in some kind of swirly floater dance. Maybe they're getting ready to attack, maybe not. I don't know and I don't care. All I care about is going into the LTT alone. I load up one pocket with my tools. In the other pocket I stash the half bag of marijuana and eight azith pills wrapped in a napkin. I think about taking the gun but decide not to. No bullets, no point. And like, who needs the extra weight? One last check on Aunt Janet. She opens her eyes, but just barely.

"I'm going in," I say.

"Good luck," she says. "I'll be right here when you come out."

Her eyes close. I shut the door.

It's time for the Pirate to visit the hotel.

- OPTION THREE -

The mini-PODs are dancing. That's the best way to describe what they do. When they first floated down it was chaos. Then they formed these black amoeba-like patches that flowed over the ground like a paint spill. Then those patches, each of which easily contained thousands of mini-PODs, merged into super-patches, which divided and merged and divided. That process went on all morning. Now they're organized into roving clusters of ten to twenty. Some individual mini-PODs within the clusters swirl around the others like partners in a square dance. Whatever the hell it is they're doing, it's an amazing thing to see. Almost as good as drugs—not that I'm an expert on that subject. I've been watching them from the kitchen table for hours.

Dad walks into the room. His hair is combed, and he's wearing a clean-looking pair of khakis and a snappy button-down shirt under a blue V-neck sweater. I wonder if he thinks he's going to work. This is a big departure from our usual assortment of grungy sweats, jeans, and winter jackets. He's carrying a shoebox-sized package wrapped in colorful paper. A pathetic attempt at a bow is taped to the top (obviously not one of Mom's works of art), along with a card in a yellow envelope. He puts the box in front of me on the table.

I say, "Dude! Look at Mr. Spiffy. What's the special occasion?"

Dad places the package in the center of the table and sits opposite me.

"Happy birthday," he says.

Happy birthday? What's up with this? Even though he's smiling I know he's dead serious. The urge to blast him with my sarcasm cannon is overpowering.

He says, "Go ahead, open it."

"You're a little late, you know."

"Sorry about that. For some reason a celebration didn't seem appropriate at the time."

"Admit it," I say. "You forgot."

He shakes his head. "This box has been in my closet the whole time. I see it every day, right there next to Mom's sweaters." He looks down at his hands. "Alien invasions have a way of...rearranging priorities."

I shrug and open the card. It's something lame about sweet sixteen and parties and being broke. I skip all that because of what I see at the bottom—Dad's signature, and below that, Mom's. I recognize her handwriting. She wrote:

> *Dear Josh, I'm so proud of you. You deserve this and more. I love you so much,*
>
> > *Mom.*

Dad wrote pretty much the same thing, but without the L-word. I couldn't read it because my eyes got all watery. It was as though I could hear her whispering the words inside my head. For the first time since all this started, I felt like she really, really, really is alive.

Dad says, "She wanted to fill out the card ahead of time, just in case she got delayed."

"Delayed, huh? That's one way to put it."

Something flashes in his eyes, like I just picked at a scab that isn't healed. I immediately wish I'd said something else. Something less like...me. "I mean, that sounds like Mom," I say. "Always thinking ahead."

"That's okay," he says, nudging the box toward me.

"Nice bow," I say.

I peel back the tape and remove the wrapping paper. It's a car stereo. Sony. AM/FM, CD, MP3 compatible, anti-theft face plate, and multicolor LCD display.

"Very cool," I say. "Finally some decent tunes for the Camry."

Dad reaches in his pocket and pulls out another box. This one is much smaller, and the wrapping is nice and tight. Definitely a Mom job. I open the box. It's the keys to the Camry.

I'm stunned.

"It was Mom's idea," he says, choking out the words. "She wanted to give it to you herself, but, well, she isn't, I mean she's not here, so... "

The man is drowning. I have to say something. "This is amazing." Despite my best efforts, my eyes continue to leak.

"We were going shopping for a new car for Mom when she got back. She was finally going to get that red convertible."

I wipe my eyes. "I guess it means you're off the hook when I miss the bus."

"That's right. No more six a.m. rides from me. But you're on your own for gas."

I'd like to keep this conversation going, but it's hard work talking about regular stuff like school and gas and car stereos and Mom when an alien brood is doing a hoedown right outside the kitchen window. I watched an apartment house full of screaming people burn to the ground, and I sent Dutch to be eaten by our neighbors. All that history builds an uncomfortable silence that could last for minutes or hours or days. But if I concentrate I hear the whisper of mini-PODs sliding through the bushes bordering our lawn.

Dad says, "Let's install it."

"The stereo?"

"Absolutely."

"In the Camry?"

"No, in the bathroom." He smiles. "Of course the Camry!" His smile spreads from ear to ear like he just invented decaf lattes or something.

"You're serious?" I say.

"Totally serious. It'll be fun."

"But why? It's totally pointless!"

"And that's *exactly* the point."

I'm sure there's some great deep meaning to what he just said, but to me it's a sign. The balding engineer with the broken nose is losing it. The mini-PODs sent him over the edge. Well, it's about time. I shrug, thinking what the hell. Why not? It's got to be better than waiting for the mini-PODs to start spraying nerve gas.

"Okay," I say. "But I get to pick the first CD."

We install the stereo after a memorable lunch of red kidney beans in mystery sauce. The job goes okay, considering that what we accomplished in an afternoon could have been done by one guy at Stereo City in thirty minutes. But to our credit, their installers don't work in a dark garage with nothing but a lilac-scented candle to help them figure out which wire is blue and which is red. Once we're done, though, I have to admit that it looks pretty sweet. Nice and tight, flush to the dash, perfect colors. I press the power button. I know what the result will be, but I can't help myself. Nada. My first stereo in my first car and I'd trade them both for a hamburger and a small fries.

Dad says, "Let's come back after dinner. You can show me your top five CDs and I'll show you mine. Then I have something I'd like to discuss with you."

I spend the time before dinner in my room figuring out my top five CDs of all time. I hear Dad go out to the garage once, probably to fill a bucket. Then I hear him in the kitchen preparing our latest feast. The pantry is nearly empty, so I'm guessing beans or corn unless he has a secret stash. I figure in a couple of days we'll resort to luring squirrels and birds into the house.

During "dinner" I ask Dad what he thinks the mini-PODs are up to.

He says, between spoonfuls of cold kidney beans, "My theory is that their home planet ran out of natural resources, so they came here. They're analyzing the ground for metals and nutrients, with the goal of setting up a trans-stellar mining operation. But you've been watching them more than I have. What's your take?"

I'm about to answer when I see something outside that catches my breath. "Check it out," I say, pointing at the window.

A coyote is walking across the field on the other side of the swamp. It approaches the cluster of PODs. They freeze, mid-dance. The coyote trots through the cluster like it's just another piece of the scenery. Once the animal emerges on the other side, the PODs go back to their mystery dance.

After the coyote vanishes over a small hill, I say, "I think the PODs are mapping the planet, getting ready to sell the real estate to rich POD pilots so they can build their POD mansions and raise their little POD families."

Dad raises his eyebrows. It's not often that I surprise him, but somehow I did this time. "I like your version better," he says. "At least that way the planet won't be sucked dry and turned into space debris. That's a future we were heading for long before the PODs arrived."

Once the feast of beans is done and the counters are sparkling clean, we head for the garage. It's time for the battle of the top fives and for our "discussion," which is Dad-code for "Here's what we're going to do." I sit in the driver's seat—it is, after all, my ride. Dad sits next to me, a small stack of CDs in his hand. I'm more of a classic alt-rock fan, so Nirvana's *Nevermind* tops my list, followed closely by their raging *In Utero*. Then it's the Pixies' *Doolittle* and *Here Comes Your Man*, and rounding out my list, the sultry *Come Away With Me* by Norah Jones, a CD I once listened to for four hours straight. No surprises with Dad. He brought the three B's: Beatles, Buffett, and Beethoven.

Once we've finished pointing out the obvious flaws in each other's lists, Dad says, out of the blue, "If I died, could you eat me?"

"*What?*" I ask, not believing what I just heard.

"I need to know. Would you be willing to eat me?"

"Would I *eat* you? Like, hack off one of your fingers and chew?"

"Yes."

"Hell, no," I say. "No way. Wait—excuse me. No *freaking* way! Would you eat me?"

"That would be impossible," he says, his eyes fixed on the dashboard.

"I can't believe we're even having this conversation. Jesus, Dad—when did you come up with that whopper?"

"No, really. I'm serious. I've been thinking a lot about this."

"Well, you can officially stop thinking about it."

"Listen to me, Josh. I should have done a better job of rationing, but as you said, what's the point? So here we are. We're down to three envelopes of powdered milk, two cans of beans, and less than half a can of corn. That's it. The water heater is almost empty. We could hope for rain, but somehow the PODs turned off the water. Plus"—and here he takes a deep breath—"my pacemaker stopped working, so the odds of me surviving even under normal circumstances aren't—"

"That's a load of crap, Dad. You could—"

"Don't interrupt me, Josh, okay? I need to say this."

The tone of his voice sets me vibrating like piano wire. He's going to say this no matter what, so I clamp my teeth and wait for him to finish talking like a lunatic.

"I could die from a heart attack tomorrow, so why waste any more food on me? One of us needs to carry on for Mom, and the only person that could be is you. And if you're willing to eat me, which I truly hope you are, then you could live for another—"

"Just forget it already! I'm not sticking a fork in you! Period! You got that? Thanks but no thanks. Come up with a different freaking plan." I can tell he's disappointed, but I'm not listening to any more of this crazy talk. "I'm outta here," I say, reaching for the door.

Dad grabs my shoulder. "Wait! Josh—there's something else I need to say."

Ninety-nine percent of me screams *Get out of the car,* but something in his eyes stops me. Like he's crossed a line and there's no return. I sit back, ready to bolt if he keeps up with the cannibalism theme.

He takes one of those deep breaths, the kind that is always followed by something profound, and says, "Remember when we were talking about which would be a better way to die, getting zapped or starving to death?"

"I picked zapped. I still do."

"There's a third option." He reaches into his coat pocket and brings out a bottle of pills.

"What are those?"

"Prescription painkillers. They're left over from when Mom hurt her back."

"That was, like, five years ago. Are they still good?"

"I took one last night. They are *very* good." He waits for my reaction.

"Go on," I say.

"There's thirty-two pills in here. That should be...enough."

"Enough for what, exactly?"

"To float off on a cloud and never wake up."

"We avoid watching each other turn into walking skeletons?"

"That's right."

"No eating human flesh?"

"Not one stringy bite."

"One question," I say. "Why this and not death by POD?"

"I'm just not sure about what happens...after."

"You think there's an 'after'?"

"Yes. I'd rather take my chances with God."

"Technically, isn't this suicide? As I recall, God is pro-life."

"I'd still rather take my chances."

It's my turn for the deep breath. "Okay," I say. "That works for me. When is this event?"

"I think we should sleep on it. If we still feel like it's the best option, then we do it after breakfast."

I'm a little uncomfortable with the speed of this...development. But I roll with it. That Dad, he's just full of surprises.

- THE SPIRAL OF LIFE -

Rat turds and spiderwebs.

I flick the lighter just enough to see where I'm going, then turn it off. All this reminds me of something Mom called the Spiral of Life. That's when things go right, they go really right. And when they go wrong, they go really wrong. Like a friend of hers at work was sad because her husband was in Iraq and she was pregnant and alone. When the baby was born it was sick and needed lots of extra medicine. But the baby got better and went home from the hospital. When the woman went back to work she got a raise. Then her husband returned from Iraq and he wasn't hurt and he wasn't crazy. Three weeks later she won fifty thousand dollars on a scratch ticket. And if that wasn't enough, she entered a sweepstakes at Home Depot and won a new kitchen. That's the Spiral of Life going up.

Then there's the spiral going the other way. Mom hooks up with a boyfriend who hits her. We bail and head for San Diego. We run out of gas and money. She leaves me and doesn't come back. The aliens come. Richie takes Cassie. I go on a rescue mission to save Cassie, but I can't reach her. So I save Aunt Janet instead, which makes me think that the spiral is finally going up. Then Richie eats Cassie. Then the aliens send billions of floaters, we don't have any food, the gun is worthless, and I have to go into the hotel alone because Aunt Janet is sick.

If I really think about it, I've been spiraling in this direction since Zack moved in. But Mom says the spiral can change direction at any time. You just have to keep your head on straight, do good things, wait your turn.

I reach the kitchen vent. There aren't any candles, but I see a thin line of light around the double doors. I push on the vent and it swings open. I slip inside, listening for sounds and ready to bolt like a deer in a forest full of hunters. At first there's nothing; then

I hear voices on the other side of the door. They're headed my way, so I climb back inside the vent head first. I wait in the dark for the door to open. It doesn't. They keep talking and I keep waiting. I think about Aunt Janet curled up and sick in the SUV. I think about Mom, wherever she is—or isn't. I focus on the Spiral of Life and think that if it's ever going to spin the other way, now would be a good time to start. Eventually my eyes close and then I'm not in this wormhole but in a place where nothing is wrong and the sun is warm and nobody has to wait for anyone.

And that place is anywhere but here.

Dad outdoes himself for breakfast. Powdered popcorn cheese is an interesting addition. It gives the red beans a disturbing layer of flavor. But not to worry—warm water with an extra helping of rust takes care of the aftertaste. We chat about movies and music. Outside, clouds gather like a storm is brewing, but it's really just a big tease. The POD commander has no intention of letting us have any water. All in all, I'd say it's a perfect day for swallowing some pills.

Breakfast takes all of ten minutes. I help Dad wipe the dishes with a towel—two bowls, two spoons. He insisted on using our good china for this meal, so that means he also insists on stacking them neatly afterward in the antique cupboard he bought Mom for her birthday, each bowl in the appropriate bowl-shaped slot. During this exercise I have a compelling desire to hurl these bowls at the wall, one by one. But why bother? As with everything else I'm doing this morning, I have to wonder if that's the way I want to leave this world—throwing meaningless dishes at a meaningless wall.

Dad wipes down the counter. He does this lovingly, as though it's a cherished pet he's putting down after twelve loyal years. I consider telling him I know about his midnight cleaning sessions, but why bother? That would be pointless. It's all so freaking pointless.

He folds and refolds the towel, hangs it on the hook. I stand by the sink, waiting for him to bring up the subject that's been swinging over our heads like a toxic piñata. Finally he runs out of stupid tasks to do.

"All right, then," he says, turning to me. "What's your position on option number three?"

I close my eyes and here's what I see: One can of beans. A dog leash without a dog. Keys to a car I'll never drive. Smoldering ashes across the street. A twisted bicycle in the cul-de-sac. I try to imagine myself gnawing on raw squirrel, but that image doesn't work. I open my eyes.

"My position on option number three," I say in a voice that's more definite than I feel, "is two thumbs up."

"Where would you like to do it?"

This question surprises me. It's a little unfair, actually. I mean, he's probably been obsessing about this important decision for days, and this is my first crack at it. I panic a little, thinking that the decision is too big. How could I possibly pick the place where I'll draw my last breath? What I need is a metaphor, something that makes a statement. And then it comes to me—the perfect spot. If Mom is alive, it's where I'd like her to find me.

"The Camry," I say.

While he's counting out the pills, I ask him what happened to his survival spirit. Why the change of heart?

"I couldn't bear to see you starve to death," he says. "And I don't trust the PODs. There might be something we don't understand about zapping, something sinister, and that possibility troubles me."

"Define 'troubles.'"

"I don't know—it's...it's...basically, I don't think those people are dead, and I don't think the PODs are taking them to heaven. The process is too clean. It reminds me of catching fish with a gill net."

"Where do you think they go?"

"I don't know. The feedlot idea sticks in my mind."

He waits for me to say something, but what can I say? Who wants to spend eternity in an alien feedlot? I think maybe I should tell him about the episodes, but decide now isn't the time.

He says, "And since you won't eat me, well, here we are."

"You got that right. A month ago when you had some meat on your butt, maybe. But now you're all scrawny and probably chewier than your two-dollar steaks."

"Mom always said I had terrible taste."

"Have you changed your mind?" I say. "Are you opting for death by jokes instead?"

He smiles, shakes the pills into his hand, then divides the pile evenly between the two of us. His hand is shaking, and mine isn't exactly steady. I stare at them in my palm. Sixteen red-and-white capsules. Sixteen tickets to an eternity I suddenly don't want to think about.

"This isn't easy for me," he says.

"I know, Dad."

Looking me dead in the eyes, he says, "You don't have to do this."

I stare at the rusty water on the dash. "I know, Dad."

"You have a choice."

"I know. I know. Really, it's all good. It's the right thing to do." My words sound confident, but my throat is tight and dry and my brain is spinning. It's like I'm riding my bike down a hill that's too steep and I can't jump off and I can't stop. At the bottom is an infinite black pit. I want to throw the pills out the window. I want to scream, *How the hell did we get here?* To grab Dad and shake him and say, *I'm afraid. Don't make me do this!* But he's not making me do this. It's all me. So here's the broken-dish moment all over again. I stare out the windshield, choosing to keep those thoughts and words inside.

Dad draws in a deep breath, lets it out. "All right, then. Let's do it."

"You first? Me first? Together? What's the game plan here?"

"How about I count to three and then we swallow them at the same time?"

"That works." I smile, but it's not easy.

He says, "I love you, Josh."

"I love you, too."

"You're a great son."

"And you're the best dad ever."

A trickle of sweat rolls down his forehead. His eyes are brimming and wet. So are mine.

I love you, Mom, wherever you are.

"One...two...three."

We swallow the pills.

At first I'm afraid there's too many, that I'll choke on them. There's a strange aftertaste, sweet like candy and bitter at the same time. He hands me the water. I take a sip, enough to do the job, and hand it back to him. He drains the glass, puts it on the dash.

Dad sits back in his seat, eyes closed. He starts talking about how he's sorry this is happening, that he and Mom are very proud of me, that he should have rationed the food better, that he's sorry about Dutch and he's sorry about punching me in the eye.

I tell him that it's all okay, that none of this is his fault. It's all the PODs. One hundred percent.

He says that being a father is the only significant thing he's ever done. That being a father is what defines him. It's really pouring out of him now. I'd like to listen, but my head is filling with helium. Pink Floyd is starting to sing. I'm a balloon and I'm starting to float.

Dad reaches out. I see that he's touching my hand, but I don't feel it.

"I'm so sorry," is all he says.

I'd like to say *Me too*, but my lips won't move.

That's my last thought before everything goes comfortably numb.

- TACO SEASONING -

I wake up in total darkness. That's no biggie. I've been doing this for so long I'm sort of used to it. My brain clock says I was sleeping for one hour twenty-two minutes. Definitely not good. Not when you're on a mission. I listen for sounds. The kitchen is quiet, and so is the hall behind the doors.

I crawl backwards out of the wormhole. Once I hit the floor I flick the lighter and look around. The box that held Cassie is gone. There are no pots boiling on the stove. I fight the urge to keep looking. It would take up minutes I don't have.

It's time to get the party started.

Aunt Janet told me what to expect on the other side of the swinging doors. There's a restaurant with tables and chairs, and some boxes of food in a corner by the windows facing the street, but the boxes are probably empty by now. On the other side of the restaurant is the door that opens into the lobby. And on the other side of that door: Black Beard. Aunt Janet said that the guards sometimes come into the restaurant for snacks and naps, so I need to be extra careful.

After five minutes of waiting next to the swinging doors and hearing nothing but my heart pounding against my ribs, I figure it's time to take a chance. I slip through the doors and ease them closed behind me. One quick peek with the lighter. Table, chairs, boxes. Nobody taking a nap. I see the shadowy shape of Black Beard through the smoky glass door. He's at his post, sitting in a chair reading a magazine.

Part 1, check. Now for Part 2.

Mom used to say that Zack made the best "liar's sandwich" she'd ever heard. That means he'd take a big fat juicy lie and slap it between two thick pieces of moldy truth, then feed it to anyone stupid enough to listen. That's how I told Aunt Janet I would get past Black Beard—I'd feed him a liar's sandwich. I take a deep breath, turn the handle, and walk right out the door.

Black Beard stands up, his magazine flying to the floor. He always looked big from a distance, but up close and personal he's huge. Almost as tall as the door and nearly as wide. Add in the beard, the long hair, and the fat, crooked nose, and he's just about the scariest, ugliest thing I've ever seen. His hand goes to the gun sticking out of his pants, but when he sees it's only a skinny little girl, he growls, "Who the hell're you?"

"I'm Megs."

"How'd you get in there?"

A wall of stink hits me in the face like a shovel. Ripe roadkill is the best way to describe it.

"I snuck in when you went to the bathroom awhile back."

Black Beard frowns for a second, his thug-sized brain chewing on that bite of the sandwich. I look around the lobby. Most people, if they're not sleeping, are at the windows watching the floaters. The parking-garage entrance is guarded by a guy I don't recognize. Where's Hacker? I look across the lobby and my stomach tightens. Richie is at his spot, the door leading down to the dark hallway. He's got the knife out, flicking it open and closed, doing that spinning trick. I feel his dark eyes under the hood aimed right at me. I don't see Mary. This means, according to Aunt Janet, that she and baby Lewis are probably on the tenth floor with her husband. Aunt Janet's words fill my head: *She'd better be in the lobby, Megs, because you absolutely don't want to go up to the tenth.*

Black Beard says, "What were you doing in there?" His eyes find my bulging pockets. "Stealing food, eh? Let's see what Señor Hendricks thinks—"

"I didn't touch the food. I was looking for the kitty. Then... then I got tired and took a nap."

"The kitty?" He laughs, his thick lips folding back to show brown teeth as big as piano keys. "The kitty is taking a nap too. A real long nap." He laughs again, then steps in close, puts one of his cigar-sized fingers under my chin, and lifts. "Why haven't I seen you before, Chiquita, hmm?" Under the stench I smell...taco seasoning?

"You've seen me," I say, pulling back. "You just don't remember."

"Oh, I never forget faces—especially one like yours."

"I spend most of the time on the tenth floor with my father."

"Your father, eh? Which one is he?"

I picture the round man I watched Richie beat up in the parking lot on the second day. "He's short and bald and used to be fat. That jerk punched him in the stomach." I point to Richie. "He almost killed him."

Black Beard nods. "I remember that punch." His thick eyebrows bunch together. "What happened to your eye?"

"I bumped it on a chair when I was hiding from him."

"Señor Badass, eh? You're not the only one," he says. His eyes soften. They slide down, focus on my pockets again. I hold my breath. How will I explain the knife, the tape, the pepper spray? I have to do something, and fast.

"Can I go now?" I say. "I need to get back to my father. He's sick and I'm not feeling very good." I cough and make sure to aim it at him and not cover my mouth.

"Sí. Sí. Go away. Stop bothering me." Black Beard picks up his magazine. A woman in a very small bikini is on the cover. She's wearing an army helmet and firing a machine gun. "But," he says, his voice dropping to a low rumble, "I wouldn't let Señor Badass see what's in your pockets." The big man turns a page and smiles. I head for the lobby, not wanting another look at those teeth.

Aunt Janet said the only way to the tenth floor is the emergency stairway located around the corner from the elevator doors. To get there I have to go right in front of Richie. As I cross the room I walk past the freckle-faced boy. He's sitting on a couch next to his twin sisters. They're playing cards. He watches me the whole time. To everyone else I'm just a ghost.

Everyone else, that is, except Richie.

I'm just about past him, my eyes aimed at the tiled floor, when he says, "The big man show you some pretty pictures?"

I know I should keep walking, but I don't. I stop, turn around, and force myself to look at him. He flips the knife open, spins it one way, then the other.

"He said you killed...you killed the kitten." I almost said "Cassie." *Don't blow it, Megs.*

Working on a fingernail with the knife, he says, "There is that rumor going around." Then he looks up. His eyes find mine. From in the shadows I see them, small and coffee-black and empty—almost. A spot of something is in there, deep, like the stuff that lurks at the bottom of a bad-luck well. It's a place I don't want to go, so I turn away.

"Look at me," he says. "Is this the face of a kitty killer?"

I focus on a scrap of paper on the floor.

"I said *look* at me!"

My head snaps up, our eyes lock. He smiles slow, like the devil getting his way.

"I said do I look like someone who would kill a helpless kitten? A kitten that was left all alone on a stinky old sleeping bag? Who would do such a thing?"

I see that spot again in his eyes. But this time I feel it, like bugs crawling down my throat. He's watching me a little too closely.

"I know you're awful and evil," I say, "if that's what you mean." I walk toward the stairway. My whole body is shaking.

"I'll take that as a yes. Be sure to say hi to the crazy Russian," he calls. Then, as I open the door: "Wanna know my secret taco recipe?"

The hike up ten flights of stairs takes just about every ounce of energy I have. Aunt Janet said there wouldn't be a guard on the door on the sixth floor because it's always locked and only Mr. Hendricks has the keys. She's right. When I reach the eighth floor the smell hits me—and it gets worse with every step. By the time I get to tenth floor I'm holding my sleeve over my nose and panting like a raced-out greyhound.

I walk through the doors and into a nightmare.

Men shuffle down the halls, skeleton-thin with sunken eyes and long, stringy hair. Clothes hang loose like curtains draped over bones. Most are sitting or lying down. It smells like a sewer and, above it all like a cloud, death. Watching it all are two men with guns, both weapons out and ready. They are staring at me with dark, suspicious eyes. One of them is Hacker. He was thin before. Now he's a stick with legs. The other guy is young, maybe eighteen, with a patchy beard and a backwards Sox baseball cap. He has a tattoo of barbed wire around his neck. They're both wearing white filters over their mouths. Hacker's has a big brownish pink stain on it.

I walk up to Hacker and say, "I'm supposed to find Mary."

"Says who?"

"Mr. Hendricks."

Hacker looks at the young guy. "You check it out, Vladi. I'm not hiking down those stairs. Not until I get some damn food."

Vladi says, "Is your turn, old man. I'm not doing stairs again."

He has an accent. I'm guessing he's the Crazy Russian.

Back to me, Hacker says, "Which one is she?"

"She has a sick baby."

"We got lotsa those—well, not as many as we used to—but I think I know who you're talking about. Down the hall..." He bursts into a powerful coughing fit. It almost knocks off his filter. Vladi shakes his head. The pink stain on Hacker's filter turns a dark red. He settles down and says, "It's on your right. She's in the room with the closed door. Ten-oh-eight, I think. But you gotta wear one a these," he says, handing me a filter, "or you don't leave this floor—ever."

All the doors down the hall are wide open. There are four to five people in each room: men, women, kids, all crammed in together. It reminds me of the time I went to the animal shelter. The same bad smell, the same sad eyes.

I come to the room with the closed door. Someone wrote *Sick People* and drew a skull and crossbones in big black marking pen under the room number, 1008. I open the door and step inside.

The air is hot and wet, almost smothering. I resist a strong urge to turn around and leave. There must be twenty people in here of all ages, but mostly kids on the two beds. Adults are in chairs or on the floor. Coughing and wheezing and the occasional whisper are the only sounds I hear. I spot the two kids I saw on the first day. They are asleep on a blanket in the corner. Next to them is a man, eyes closed, skin the color of a dirty sheet, slumped against a wall. I'm not sure if he's alive or dead, but I have a pretty good guess. I should know a bloater when I see one.

I recognize Mary the second I see her. She's the one I saw though the vent—tall, with red hair. She's sitting in a chair, legs straight out in front of her, staring at the open window. Baby Lewis is wrapped in a yellow blanket and sleeping on her lap.

I walk to her, stepping over and around the people as I go. Some stare at me. Most don't care. I look out the window. The view is insane. The streets of Los Angeles, lit up under a warm morning sun, look like a pulsing black river of floaters flowing in all directions. Straight ahead, in the distance, the street ends in a boiling mountain of smudgy whites and grays with flashes of light inside. It's beautiful in a freakish sort of way, like a storm cloud fell from the sky. If I were in a car headed toward that thing, I'd be screaming at the driver to turn around.

"What is it?" I ask, pointing at the mystery cloud. I hear a throaty rattling sound. Baby Lewis moves, then stops.

Without turning her head, Mary says, "It's supposed to be a view of the ocean. They took that away, too."

"How long has it been there?"

This time she does look at me. Her eyes, sunken deep in shadowy pockets, narrow in suspicion. "Since day two. Where have you been?"

Someone whispers behind me. I lean toward her, my mask close to her ear. "This is from Carrie." I hand her the napkin with the azith pills inside. "It's an antibiotic. Aunt Janet—I mean Carrie—says to dissolve a quarter pill in a cup of water. Three times a day until they're gone."

She quickly stashes the package in the folds of the blanket. "Carrie's alive? I thought she—"

I bring my finger to the mask. "Shh." I nod, *Yes*.

"We won't get water until tomorrow afternoon."

A voice from behind says, "I've never seen her before."

I slide the half bag of marijuana into Mary's lap, using my hand to keep it hidden from prying eyes. She looks at the package, not sure what to think. Then, figuring it out, she asks, "Where'd you get this?"

"Maybe your husband can use it to bribe the guards for water."

Her eyes mist over. I can tell she's about to cry. Definitely not good. "My husband died last night."

I think of the man slumped against the wall. I'd like to say something, but this conversation has to end.

"Who are you?" she chokes out.

But I'm already moving. Weaving my way to the door, reaching for the handle. Someone grabs my shoulder from behind. A voice wheezes, "Hey, you can't—"

I twist down and away, then I'm out the door. I head for the stairway, breathing hard through my mask, walking fast but not too fast. I'm just about there when Vladi yells from down the hall, "Hey! Stop!"

Should I run? Go for it? It's ten floors. He'd probably catch me. And he has a gun. He might figure things out and take the pills from Mary.

Walking toward me, Vladi says, "You must to give me something."

My brain is screaming, *Run!* I wrap my fingers on the door handle.

"Not so fast," he says. I smell him behind me. Then he's touching my hair. I look to my left. Hacker's eyes are smiling, like he's seen this before. Like he's about to have some fun. I let go of the door. My hand creeps inside the pocket with the pepper spray. Vladi whispers in my ear, "I let you go, little girl," he says, "after you give me something."

My fingers find the can, search for the top.

He says, "Give me mask. Then you go."

I fly down the stairs, realizing that I have no plan. My mind races through the options as I run. The kitchen escape route—blocked by Black Beard. The access door on floor six—locked. The lobby access door—guarded. The door to the long, dark hall—Richie. The hotel lobby entrance—alien death ray. There's no way out. By the time I reach the bottom floor I'm like a hamster running on a wire wheel, totally exhausted and totally trapped. I can't just stay in the hotel. Sooner or later someone will figure out that no one recognizes me and tell Richie or Mr. Hendricks, hoping to trade food or water for the information. Or even worse, Richie figures it out by himself, which means all kinds of bad news for me, and probably for Mary and the baby. Like Zack would say to Mom, *Sure you have options, but they're all bad.* I decide my best play is to do what I do best: hide and wait. So I go out the door, turn the corner, and...

Richie isn't there.

He's on the other side of the lobby arguing with Black Beard. They're really into it, Richie poking an angry finger in the big man's chest, Black Beard smiling but not really. The door to the long, dark hall is unguarded. It's ten feet from where I stand. There's maybe twenty people in the lobby, but only one seems aware of me. It's that freckle-faced boy again. I take a couple of steps. He's definitely watching me. I put my head down and walk toward the door. Richie and Black Beard are still at it, Richie yelling that he's as stupid as a sack of hammers. I'm at the door, pressing down on the crash bar. Two seconds later and I slip like a shadow into the hall. I guide the door until it clicks softly behind me.

The hall is dark, but I remember my way. The garbage can, the fire extinguisher, a right turn, six doors down—all locked. The next door should be the utility room. It swings open, the piece of tape still where I left it. I peel off the tape, which gives me an idea. I tear it into small pieces, jam them into the lock, dart inside, and pull the door closed. It may not stop Richie, but it will definitely slow him down.

There's light framing the bottom of the exit door. My eyes adjust to the darkness enough so that I can make out shadowy shapes. The ladder is under the access vent, but something isn't right. The vent cover is on the floor. That's not where we left it. Someone has been in here after us. And whoever it was, they chose not to take the tape off the lock. I walk quickly across the small room, then stop and listen. No sound. I open the door enough to stick my head outside. The stairway is clear and empty. I remember the look in Richie's eyes, and that crawling-insect feeling returns. My escape has been too easy, too smooth. But as far as I know, he's still fighting with Black Beard. I take a breath and walk up the stairs.

The first thing that hits me is the air. It smells...different. Maybe it's because I spent too much time in the sickroom, or too many hours in the LTT, but the air has a cool crispness to it that feels good in my lungs. I can't get enough of it. I still see a couple of floaters outside but nowhere near as many. I don't remember seeing them leave. Where did they all go?

There's no sign of Aunt Janet. I hope she's sleeping in the SUV. I take a step in that direction—

An arm wraps around my neck and jerks me off my feet.

A raspy voice whispers in my ear, "So the pirate is a *girl*. Ain't that a bitch!"

I can't breathe. The tendons in his arm feel like ropes digging into my throat. I kick my legs and try to scream. Nothing comes out but a pathetic squeak.

"Feels like your lungs are on fire, don't it? Like your eyeballs are gonna pop right out of your head?"

I can't reach my pocket to get the pepper spray. I try to scratch at his skin, reach back to gouge his eyes. He laughs. I'm starting to black out. My arms are losing their strength.

"You fight worse 'n your scrawny little cat!"

Richie throws me to the ground. I fall like a broken doll, struggling to take in ragged gulps of air. He walks over to me, looks down from underneath that hood with those black empty eyes. There's a car about ten feet away. Maybe I can get underneath it long enough to catch my breath, get out the pepper spray. I start crawling. He kicks me with his boot, knocks me over. I start crawling again. He reaches down, wraps an arm around my chest, and scoops me up. He walks toward the exit, carrying me against his hip. A floater cruises by. My arms are pinned to my side. The pepper spray, six inches from my right hand, is useless.

I try to scream. All I manage is a hoarse "Help me!"

"See, there's an art to squeezing a throat just enough so it spasms. That way they can sort of breathe, but they can't talk." He laughs. "Best invention ever. You know where I learned it? From a cop that tried to strangle me."

He drops me to the ground, pins me with his boot.

"Check this out," he says.

I look up. He folds back the hood. I see his face for the first time. His hair is black and spotty like it only grows in patches. There's a curving white scar from his forehead to the middle of his right cheek. And there's just a dark purple lump where his right ear should be.

He picks me up and says, "Yeah, yeah, I know what you're thinking. Well, you should've seen the cop."

We're almost at the exit. Three more floaters are spinning in the street.

"These things are amazing. How do they always know when it's time to eat? A minute from now they'll be swarming like ants on ice cream. I mean, it's not like I'm ringing a dinner bell." He squeezes me, hard. "Hell, you're so damn bony they may just lose their appetite. But I wouldn't bet the farm on it."

We're at the exit. The floaters are a car length away. There's a crowd of them now, spinning like evil tops about a foot off the ground. I go limp, hoping that Richie will have to adjust his grip. He shifts his arm just enough for me to sink my right hand into my pocket.

"Did you know the mother ships are com-mu-ni-cating with me?

I'm one of their whatcha- call-its...a disciple! I bring them sacrific-
es. Thanks to me, we get to survive a little longer. But do I get any
credit for saving the human race? My work is so misunderstood."

The pepper spray is in my right hand. I'll have to be quick. I
won't get a second chance. I dig the fingernails of my free hand
into his arm.

He laughs. "You think a little scratch is gonna work on me?"

But his grip loosens for just a second. That's all I need. I twist
out of his arm, land on my feet, and bring out the can, spraying as
I go. But he's faster than me. He blocks the spray with one hand,
grabs the canister with the other, and yanks it away. The air burns
with the smell and my eyes sting, but Richie is untouched. He tosses the can into the street. The floaters swarm over it.

I have nowhere to go. I'm on the edge of the exit. Two steps
back and I'm in the street. It's floaters or death rays; either way
I'm gone. Richie is blocking me from escaping into the garage. He
wipes his hands on his pants. Water leaks from his eyes. I try to
dart past him, but he grabs my shirt, pulls me back. I'm amazed at
how fast and strong he is.

He pushes me toward the street. It's jammed with floaters.

"Where's the gun?" he says.

Even if I wanted to, I wouldn't tell him. He'd feed Aunt Janet
to the aliens for sure.

"I'll bet you're hiding it with that little bitch friend of yours,
the one you *stole* from me."

Stall for time. Figure something out. That's the only plan I
have.

My voice is coming back. I could scream, but what good will
that do? I say, "I...I don't remember."

"Maybe this'll help."

There's that sickening chicken-bone click. Like magic, the
knife is in his hand. He does the spinning move around his finger.
Even in the shadows the blade seems to shine.

"Now I'm only gonna ask nice one more time. Listen close, my
little friend. Where...is...the...gun?"

"It's behind you," says a calm, familiar voice.

Richie reaches out, pins me against his body, and turns toward the sound.

Aunt Janet steps from behind a cement column. She stands maybe twenty feet away, arms out straight, holding the gun with both hands. Her target seems to be Richie's chest, about four inches above my head.

The gleaming blade is one inch from my throat.

"Let her go," she says, her eyes never leaving his.

"Why would I do that?" he says.

"Because I'll kill you if you don't."

"You kill me? That's perfect!" He takes a step toward her. "You know what I think?" The gun is shaking in her hand. Richie takes another step, pushes me forward. More shaking from Aunt Janet. The stink from Richie's arm, a mix of sweat and pepper spray, burns my nose.

Aunt Janet says, "I don't care what you think." She adjusts her stance. I know the gun is empty, but does Richie? Can he tell just by looking at it?

Richie says, "I think you got yourself a little situ-a-tion here. Just like in the movies."

He takes another step. She's really shaking now, all the way down to her legs.

"There's no point in this getting ugly, right? Hell, I bet that thing isn't even loaded."

Her face clouds. I know that look. She's fighting one of those cramps.

"So, my friend, here's how we're going to do this..."

Another step. We're fifteen feet away and closing.

He points the knife at her and says, "You're going to give me the gun, then you're—"

The shaking stops. Aunt Janet's shooting hand is as steady as a rock. Richie freezes.

I twist down and away from the blade. As I'm moving there are two quick explosions. Richie shudders like he was kicked. He lets go of my shirt, I lunge out and away. He stumbles backwards toward the street, clutching at his right shoulder with his left hand. There's red seeping out from the bottom edge. He's starting to get his balance back, rage filling his eyes.

I charge at him. He swings the knife at my head, but it's slow and easy to duck. I ram my arms into his chest, pushing him backwards with everything I've got. He stumbles, tries to stand up—but can't. Screaming, he falls into a sea of floaters. They swarm over him. There's an arm, a foot, another short scream.

Three seconds and Richie isn't Richie anymore.

I stare at Aunt Janet. She stuffs the gun into her waistband.

"What just happened?" I ask, still not believing what I saw.

She walks over, gives me a long hug. Then she steps back, looks at me, and says, "You remember when I told you there weren't any bullets?"

"Yeah."

There's a hint of a smile in her eyes. "I lied."

- BATHTUB MAN -

It takes me a few heartbeats to figure things out.

I'm in the Camry. A bright light streams in through a side window in the garage. It's so intense I have to turn away. My mouth feels like I've been sucking on cotton balls. My legs are covered with the green blanket from my bed—how did that get there? All this information is confusing enough, but it doesn't come close to answering the two questions that are burning a hole in my brain.

Number one: Why am I alive?

Number two: Why am I alone?

Last thing I remember, Dad and I swallowed a boatload of pain pills. In fact, the now-empty glass that we used to wash down the pills is still on the dashboard, right where Dad put it. I remember feeling numb, drifting off, Dad mumbling all that emotional stuff you expect to hear on your deathbed. But here I am, alive and alone. Alone in my very own 1997 gunmetal-blue Toyota Camry with 197,000 miles and a brand-new kick-ass stereo in the dash.

I can think of only two explanations. Well, three, I guess. Either I'm dreaming—but you don't have headaches in dreams, so that's definitely out—or for some reason the pills didn't work. They sure *felt* like they worked. Explanation number three, that Dad secretly owns and knows how to operate a stomach pump and wasn't too drugged to use it, is about as likely as me growing a second head. I'm going with the pills not working, which means Dad is still alive. Which also explains why I'm alone. So where the hell is he? In the house, probably fixing breakfast. Oh yeah, there is no breakfast. So he's in the kitchen counting PODs and drawing graphs. Or equally productive, cleaning the counter.

I walk into the house. The shades are down, so there's none of the blinding POD light in here. Only a soft yellow glow filtering in through the beige cloth.

I yell, "Yo, Dad! Nice job with the pills!"

I wait. No answer. Okay, be that way.

I follow that up with "Next time, read the bottle!"

Still nothing. He could be upstairs taking a nap, but this isn't a big house, and I yelled loud enough to wake the dead. A voice in my brain is whispering PODs. Like, he went to them, or worse, they came to us.

My heart speeds up a beat. This is beginning to feel like the horror movie where you want to scream at the guy on the screen, "Get out of the house, you idiot! Get out of the house!" Only in this case I'm the idiot and exiting the house is not an option.

I check out all the usual suspects: Dad's black leather chair in the den, the couch in the living room, the dining room chair facing the window, the kitchen.

All spotless, all empty. My eyes drift to the wooden block of butcher knives. Something seems wrong. I look closer. The biggest knife, the one Dad uses for carving a turkey, is gone. He has a hissy fit when someone doesn't put it back in the block. This isn't making any kind of sense. I whip out the meat cleaver. I mean, that's what the idiot would do, right?

I walk up the stairs that now seem to have an eerie squeak. And of course there aren't many windows, so it's darker than downstairs. The meat cleaver makes my shadow especially big and menacing. I'd laugh if my teeth weren't chattering.

"Dad," I say, in a voice barely more than a whisper, "whatever it is you're doing, it's time to stop."

I'm at the top of the stairs. The hall goes left, to my room, or right, to the master bedroom. Dad's door is wide open. Nap or no nap, he should hear me. My door is closed, so that's where I go first. Even though it's my room, I feel the urge to knock.

I tap my knuckles on the white wood and say, "Dad, you in there? Dad?"

He doesn't answer. I turn the knob and step inside.

All my stuff is put away. The bookcase is organized, my desk is clear, my clothes are folded and stacked on the dresser. My shoes are paired up and in a tidy row under the window. My bed looks so perfect it could be in a Marriott ad. And on top of that perfect, wrinkle-free bed is a white envelope with my name on it.

I put the meat cleaver on the windowsill, knowing that this is the point in the movie where the psycho jumps out of the closet. Strange thing is, I'm more afraid of this envelope than I am of closet psychos or POD storm troopers. My hands shake as I tear open the flap. There's a letter inside. I recognize Dad's meticulous engineer-style handwriting. His voice echoes in my head as I read.

> *Dear Josh –*
>
> *If you're reading this letter, that means you survived. Great! Believe it or not, that's my plan. Two of your pills were pain pills. The rest were filled with powdered milk. It wasn't a mean trick. I did this because I'm your father. I know I'm being selfish, but I want you to live. This invasion won't last forever. Mom may still be alive. If there's even a small chance that you can survive to the "after" when the PODs leave, you should take it.*

A tear falls on the paper. It makes a dark, wet stain.

> *I'm hoping you change your mind about what we discussed earlier. Eating me is the right thing to do. But you can't think about it for very long; otherwise the meat will spoil. I also understand if you can't do it. It's a tough decision—one you have to make alone. All I ask is that you please don't toss my carcass to the PODs. I'm in the master bath either way. I love you.*
>
> *Dad*

> *PS: The drugs from your pills are in a baggie under the book on my nightstand. But use it only at your darkest hour. <u>Don't</u> let the PODs take you. I don't trust them.*

The *meat* will spoil? *Carcass?* Just thinking about those words makes my stomach flip. I'm crying so hard I can hardly breathe. But maybe he's still alive. Maybe I can stop him!

I crash through the doorway, sprint down the hall and into Dad's bedroom. More of that bright light is pouring in through the window. The bathroom door is closed. I yell, "Dad!" and kick my way in.

He's in the bathtub, naked except for his black boxers. There's a skylight in the ceiling above him. A rectangle of sunlight stretches across his motionless face. I can tell he's dead. The chalky white skin, the stiffness, the silence—I just know it. There's no point in taking his pulse. My father is dead.

I drop to the floor. I'm not crying now. Whatever I was feeling when I read the letter, when I was running down the hall, crashing through doors—it's been replaced by something else. Like I'm freezing from the inside out. I focus on a blue towel hanging on a hook. The toilet seat, a toothbrush on the sink. Anything to keep my eyes from the awful, silent truth that fills this room.

My father is dead.

I'm not.

Now I'm all alone.

Those three sentences seep into the silence and fill the cracks. They repeat themselves in an endless, building loop. My body starts to shake. Tears come again, this time in long, shuddering waves. Then it passes like a storm and all is quiet again. I take a deep breath. Slowly turn my head.

His hands are folded across his pale stomach. They're holding a picture of the three of us, and Dutch, at Cannon Beach in Oregon. We went there for spring break last year. I remember the moment exactly. Mom bought a ten-dollar kite from a sidewalk vendor. The stupid thing just refused to fly. We ran up and down the beach like idiots, Dutch barking his head off every time it crashed in the sand. There was an old Chinese guy fishing in the surf. She offered to give him the kite if he took our picture. He took the picture but wouldn't take the kite. It's still hanging on a nail in the garage.

I sit on the edge of the tub and look down at him. For a second I get this feeling like he's in a coffin and I'm at his funeral. Only his casket is white porcelain and has a drain. His eyes are closed and his face is calm, almost smiling. His nose is still a little bluish and puffy. I reach out to touch him but can't swing the final inch. He looks cold, so I cover his body with a towel. One of my fingers brushes his skin. I shiver.

On the corner of the tub is another envelope, one I've been avoiding. He wrote in big black letters on the front: INSTRUCTIONS. Under the envelope, the missing knife.

I pick up the envelope. This is nuts. Instructions for what? I can only imagine. I tear it in half, crush the pieces into tight balls, and heave them against the wall. With each movement I feel my body filling with that blackness. The PODs. They did this. They put my father in this tub. They made him lie to me. They made him write a letter with INSTRUCTIONS at the top.

Dad said there are more pills on his nightstand. Why put off the inevitable? Then I think, screw the pills. Even though he asked me not to, I'm going to settle this outside. I crave that one blissful release before it all ends in a flash of light.

But I have to do this fast, before the rage turns to stone.

I leap down the stairs two at a time, open the door, run outside, and scream, "COME AND GET ME, YOU MOTHER—"

It's gone. The POD across the street is gone.

I look to the west, over the elementary school, where a POD has lurked since day one. Not there. The sky is perfectly clear. In fact, it's a color of blue I've never seen before. Intense, not washed out or hazy. Like a crayon fresh out of the box. I run to the side yard. The pile of waste is gone, like it was never there. The sky is clear of PODs for as far as I can see. And I can see a long way. There are snowcapped mountains in the distance I didn't even know existed.

The air smells different. I close my eyes and take a breath. Warm and earthy, like the middle of a forest after a hard rain. I can almost taste it. Thinking of rain reminds me that I'm thirsty. Suddenly all I can think about is the swamp. Even if it's sewage, I'll drink it. But when I look at the water, it's clear. Like a mountain stream. Like water out of the tap, only way better. I drink until my stomach hurts.

I walk back to the front yard, make my way across the cul-de-sac. The pavement is so clean it shines. There are no cigarette butts, no scraps of paper or plastic grocery bags or pieces of broken glass. Jamie's bike is still there, but her helmet and the newspapers are gone. Someone in the distance is calling out a name. Amy, Ashley, something like that. Another voice, farther away, joins in.

I reach the street, scan left and right. All that's left of the apartment building is a few charred hunks of wood and part of a stairway. Alex's house—nothing but the corner of a standing wall with a single blackened window. Way down the block a woman I don't recognize is sitting on the curb, head in her hands. I shout, "Hey!" She lifts her head, spots me, and waves. I wave back. I start to walk toward her, then hear something that makes my heart stop. Muffled, almost not there. I know what it is, and I run toward it.

The Conrads' front door is locked. Dutch is in there, barking. I'm calling his name and slamming my shoulder into the door, but it won't budge. I switch to the living room window, which is covered with plywood. It breaks on the second try. I climb in. Dutch is all over me. Licking my face, tail wagging at the speed of light. Beyond him is a mountain of dried dog food on the kitchen floor.

I call out for the Conrads. There's no sign of them. If they were in the house I'd be seeing them by now. POD meat is my guess. But who knows. After the bathtub scene I just went through, it occurs to me that maybe they chose a way out other than being zapped or starving to death. Maybe they have their own stash of pills, or even a gun. I'll save that discovery for another time.

I'm sitting in the yard outside my house. The grass is cool, the sun is warm. Tulips are starting to poke up like green spears through the dirt in Mom's flower spot. A squirrel dashes across the grass. I glance at Dutch, wondering if he'll go nuts, but he doesn't. That's a first. I hold him by the muzzle and stare straight into his eyes. I do this sometimes when I'm stressed. Maybe it's the total trust I see there, or the absolute unawareness of how crappy things may be around him. Whatever the reason, it calms me down. I need to think. It's time to process my new reality.

My father is upstairs in the bathtub. He's dead. He'll never see what I'm seeing now.

A wave of panic stirs inside me; the emotions start to boil. At first I think it's an episode, but that changes when one more tear leaks out. I wipe it away. Dutch nudges my hand with his nose. He studies me with those curious brown eyes. Whatever demons were rising in my chest are still—for now. Dutch nudges me again. I can't help but smile.

"Well, you're the only friend I have," I say. "What are we going to do?"

I scratch the spot behind his ears. He rolls onto his back, begging for a belly rub. In his simple world, that's all that matters. But the world I knew one month ago is smashed to pieces. What's left is scattered like dry leaves in the wind. Will we ever put the pieces back together? Then I wonder about Mom. Is she looking out at the same amazing blue sky? Dad believed she's still alive. I want to believe he's right. Los Angeles isn't that far away. At least it wasn't *before* the PODS. But this is *after*. Should I go or should I stay?

"You feel like going on an adventure?" I say.

Dutch licks his nose and thumps his tail.

That would be a yes.

- THE GIFT -

Yelling, from *outside*.

We're in the cave. Aunt Janet is sleeping. I was asleep, but I'm not anymore. I'm wide awake and wondering what the heck is going on. I poke my head out of the hatch and listen. It's definitely coming from *outside* the parking garage.

Somebody yells, as clear as a bell, "They're gone! They're gone! We kicked their alien asses! The sonsabitches are gone!"

There's only one thing he could be talking about, but I have to see for myself. I jump out of the smashed Suburban, run to the side of the garage. My eyeballs almost pop out of my head. People are coming *out* of the buildings. Some are running, some are staggering like zombies. They're falling to their knees and kissing the ground. They're dancing with each other in the street. They're looking up at the sky and shaking their fists and shouting words I can't repeat. And the best part of all—the only round object in the sky is a big, warm, yellow sun. And the only thing floating in that sea of blue is clouds. Huge, white, puffy clouds. Not a single mother ship, or floater, anywhere.

Part of me thinks it could be a trick. Maybe the aliens have some kind of invisibility shield. Or maybe they landed somewhere and the real invasion is happening *right now*, just when we think it's safe to go outside. They softened us up by destroying our military and starving us half to death. Now it's just a matter of time before their bug-eyed armies march down the street firing their death rays. I blink that thought away. It definitely *feels* like they left. I have to wake up Aunt Janet. This is the best news ever.

Then I hear another sound.

Breaking glass. Lots of it. A man and a woman walk out of a building across the street. The man is carrying a chair. He throws the chair through the front window of the coffee shop next door.

He climbs in through the shattered hole. Seconds later he's opening the door from the inside. The woman disappears into the shop with him. They come out a minute later holding paper sacks full of something. I don't know what for sure, but I'm guessing it's food. The woman hurries inside for more. The man reaches into his sack and pulls out a bottle of water. Other people see this and run over. Soon there's a crowd of people pushing and shoving to get inside.

I run back to the cave and shake Aunt Janet's leg. "Wake up, wake up!"

She groans something about letting her sleep.

I shake her leg harder. "The aliens are gone! People are outside. You have to come look!"

Her head pops up in the dark. "What did you say?"

"Can't you hear the shouting? People are breaking *into* buildings."

She looks at me like I'm speaking Martian. It shouldn't be this hard to make someone understand that the monsters have left the building. I tell her what's really on my mind.

"We have to get out there *now* before all the food is gone. If you don't want to come," I say, backing out of the cave, "then you can wait here and I'll bring you a doughnut—if there are any left."

"A doughnut?"

"With chocolate frosting and sprinkles."

"This better not be some trick to get me up," she says. She crawls out of the cave and follows me to the spot where I watched the man break the window. By this time the group has moved on. All that's left is some guy eating coffee beans out of a bag. There are a few more people up and down the street. Some carry paper sacks, some push grocery carts full of bags and boxes. They seem to be mostly headed in one direction.

"My God," Aunt Janet says. "It's true. They're gone!" She hugs me. Tears are rimming her eyes. "We did it. We survived."

We run down to Level 1 and stop on the sidewalk. We're standing on almost the exact spot where Richie disappeared yesterday in a swarm of floaters. Now I'm outside, with nothing over my head except blue sky. I keep expecting to see people disappear in flashes of light. I take a deep breath. The air is clear and cool and tastes of salt—and something else. Whatever that something is, I can't get enough of it.

Someone with a grocery cart full of stuffed plastic bags and a television yells, "Get the hell out of the way!"

The freckle-faced kid from the hotel is standing with his mom and two sisters in the middle of the street. The mother is cradling one of the sisters in her arms, trying to hold the limp body up but struggling under the weight. "Do you have some food? Some water?" she says to the few people that come near them. Her voice is all screechy and starting to break.

A teenage girl is walking beside an older man with a bad limp. They both have pillowcases bulging at the seams. He's carrying a baseball bat. They stop next to the woman. The man puts down his case, opens it, pulls out a bottle of water, hands it to the woman. The girl watches, shaking her head. The man says to the woman, "Do what you have to do. Don't worry about breaking the law, 'cause there ain't none." He shoulders his load and says, "An' don't take your eyes off your kids. Not for an instant." They melt into the flow.

I look where they're headed. A green-and-white street sign says Santa Monica. It's the same street I saw from Mary's window. It ended in that strange boiling cloud. But the cloud is different. Now it's light gray, like a thick wall of harmless fog that probably will burn off in the morning sun.

Aunt Janet grabs my arm. "It's *him!*" she says, pointing.

I follow her hand. My skin gets that creeping-spider feeling. Mr. Hendricks is standing in front of the hotel watching the scene from behind dark sunglasses. He's a vision of health compared to the stream of sagging bodies—well-fed, face shaved, hair trimmed and slicked back. Black Beard walks out of the hotel and stands next to him. Vladi is right behind him, the gun handle showing above his belt. He steps into the street and starts running like he needs to get somewhere fast. There's no sign of Hacker. Mr. Hendricks and Black Beard watch together as their prison empties.

Aunt Janet says to me, "Have you seen Mary?"

"No. I mean, not yet."

The sound of shuffling feet and breaking glass is all around us.

I say, "Shouldn't we find some food?"

Eyes on Mr. Hendricks, she says, "In a minute."

She's a missile locked on target. I'm two steps behind her. Black Beard sees us coming, points and whispers to Mr. Hendricks. Mr. Hendricks turns toward us and smiles, showing those big white teeth. I wonder if Aunt Janet left the gun in the SUV. We stop in front of him.

"Well, hello, aspirin thief. I see you survived to witness this historic day. And you brought the parking-garage pirate with you! This is a truly a special occasion."

Aunt Janet says, "Where is she?"

"Don't I get a 'Good morning' first?"

Aunt Janet's face is hard as a gravestone.

Still with that smile, he says, "To which of my sixty-three surviving guests are you referring?"

"You know."

"The woman with the sick infant?"

"Her name is Mary."

"Ah, yes. Your little drug dealer," he says, nodding to me, "gave Mary a half-kilo of weed, which she traded to one of my guards for a bottle of water. He coughed himself to death last night in a blissful haze of marijuana smoke."

Aunt Janet blinks, then says, "What did you do to her?"

"What happened to your friend is nothing compared to what the two of you did to Mr. Smith." Mr. Hendricks aims those sunglasses at me. His smile shifts into something small and tight, like he's considering an interesting problem for the first time. "See, my associate here, Señor Manny, witnessed the whole thing. You pushed that poor soul into the street to be shredded by those awful floating basketballs." He stays on me for a second, then returns to Aunt Janet. The smile is gone. "But lady, you shot him first, and that is a very big problem for me."

"He had a knife to her throat."

"So I'm told. Sounds like a matter of perspective to me."

"Where is Mary?"

"My, aren't you the persistent one! She was among the first guests to leave...excuse me, *check out*...this morning. And without paying her bill, I might add."

Something catches my eye down the street. People are pointing, stopping to stare. The fog is beginning to thin. A long, shadowy shape is inside. I look at Black Beard. He sees it too.

Mr. Hendricks says, "See, in the good old days I would arrest both of you for murder, then trust a judge and jury to decide your fate. But this is a brave new world. Disorder and chaos are the rule—"

There's a sharp popping sound, like a firecracker, only I know it's not. It's followed by three more fast popping sounds, one after the other. Someone yells. It's close. Maybe a couple of blocks away.

Mr. Hendricks says, "That should be Vladimir securing the pawn shop on Wilshire. The last thing we need is a bunch of crazy civilians running around with guns. Which brings me back to our situation." He leans in close to Aunt Janet and says, "I'll forget you killed my employee, on one condition: you give me the gun."

Aunt Janet waits a moment and says, "What gun?"

The big man steps back and smiles.

Mr. Hendricks says, "Then we will see each other again. Under less...celebratory circumstances, I'm afraid."

Aunt Janet turns to Black Beard and says, "Did you see which way she went?"

Black Beard looks at Mr. Hendricks. He nods. Black Beard raises a heavy arm and points down Pico Boulevard. "She wanted to head for the city. I told her the coast would be safer. I said to break into the restaurants on the pier."

The black shape is almost entirely visible. It's huge. I'm not sure "safer" is a word I would use.

Mr. Hendricks says, "See, there's your answer! She went to the beach." He shrugs. "Where else would one go in LA on a beautiful day like this?"

I dig my toes into the warm sand. Aunt Janet cradles baby Lewis in her lap and coos while he makes tiny fists with little pink fingers. Mary grinds up one of the azith pills, mixes it with water in a plastic bottle with a rubber nipple, and gives it to the baby. While he latches on and goes to town, I think about how lucky we are.

We found them under the pier sixty-seven minutes ago. Mary was hiding behind a rock, wet and shivering, with baby Lewis wrapped in a towel on her lap. She cried hard when we found her. She thought Richie had killed Aunt Janet for sure. When we told her what really happened, how Aunt Janet shot him in the shoulder and I pushed him into the street full of floaters, she laughed. Then we helped her walk to this sheltered place on the beach, gave her some dry clothes, and set up camp.

My backpack is full of canned fruits and bottled water. Aunt Janet and I scavenged them from an empty apartment above a surf shop two blocks from the beach. Mary is sitting next to a small garbage bag stuffed with instant coffee, tea, and two blankets Black Beard gave us from the hotel. We decided to stay away from the restaurants, which were crazy with starving people fighting over boxes of cereal and Hostess Ho Hos. We saw one grocery store set on fire. There's smoke from other fires rising on the horizon. I'm not sure where we'll find food when we run out of what we've got.

A pile of driftwood is at my feet, enough to last the night. We'll sleep in shifts. Aunt Janet has the gun. She says there are fourteen rounds left. I believe her—this time.

The sun is sinking low on the horizon. The sky is an amazing smear of orange, blue, and eggplant purple. Aunt Janet and Mary are talking about how clean everything is—the beach, the water, the air, even the streets, once you get past all the broken glass and the fires. All I know is, I swam in the ocean for the first time and it was clear and salty and cold as ice.

And Mom wasn't there to see me.

We left another note on the car, this one telling her to meet us at the beach at the bottom of Santa Monica. Aunt Janet and Mary agreed to stay for three days to see if she shows up. We're hoping the cell phones are working soon, but the odds aren't good. We spoke to a guy who said nothing works, not a damn thing, not even his watch. He told us to get out of the city. He said that what's going on now is nothing compared to what will happen when the shock wears off. "Once folks believe the aliens are really gone," he said, "it's going to get ugly, and fast."

Aunt Janet thinks the man is right. But her mind is on other things. She's anxious to hear from her family. She has a husband and fifteen-year-old son in Washington State. Her plan is to head north along the coast, maybe on a bicycle if she hasn't found a car that starts by then. She said she'd like me to come with her. I said I'll think about it, but I already know what I'll say. Aunt Janet needs someone to watch her back.

The sun is nearly set. Aunt Janet uses my lighter to start the fire. Mary puts a pot of water on to boil. People are doing the same all up and down the beach. Small dots of yellow flicker against the dark shimmering skin of the ocean. This seems to be the gathering place, and I know why.

The aliens left something behind.

It's a giant tower, smooth and black like the floaters. No windows, cracks, or seams that we can see. It rises out of the ocean a half mile away and brushes the clouds. Aunt Janet calls it The Monolith. Mary thinks it may be the tallest thing on the planet. Whatever it is, Aunt Janet said that the minute she saw it, the pain in her stomach went away. The closer we got, the better she felt. Her headaches and nausea were totally gone by the afternoon. And baby Lewis is getting better by the minute.

But I feel uneasy, like the tower could open any second. We'll hear that awful sound and the floaters will come pouring out and this time we won't be inside a parking garage or next to a hotel. We'll be out in the open, sleeping on a blanket under the stars. A flash of light and we'll be gone. I keep this thought to myself. But that doesn't mean I haven't been looking for places for us to hide, just in case.

Mary hands me a cup of tea. The steam smells like oranges and feels warm against my skin. Aunt Janet pokes at the fire with a stick. Sparks spiral up into a star-filled sky. She leans back, arranges the blanket over her legs, closes her eyes. In the distance someone is playing guitar and singing "Amazing Grace." It mixes with the steady drum of the ocean waves.

"Good night, Pirate," she says.

Good night. I like the sound of that.

I settle in for the first watch, my eyes locked on The Monolith.

It's going to be a long night.

Like Mom used to say, never trust gifts from a stranger.

LaVergne, TN USA
17 August 2010
193646LV00002B/2/P